# HILL

## ANTHO

## VOLUME TWO

HILLFIRE PRESS

HILLFIRE ANTHOLOGY · VOLUME 2

Hillfire Press Ltd
Enterprise Hub
11 Crichton Street
EH8 9LE

Published in 2023

Design and typesetting by Anna O'Connor
Cover illustration by Anna O'Connor

Typeset in Hightower and Iowan Old Style

Printed in the UK

ISBN: 978-1-7396226-1-9

hillfirepress.com

# HILLFIRE PRESS

*Founder, Editor-in-Chief*
Lena Kraus

*Executive Editor*
Zala Jambrovic Hatic

*Art Director*
Anna O'Connor

*Copy Editors*
Lauren N. Thurman
Miriam Huxley

*Digital Marketers*
Zala Jambrovic Hatic
Lola Gaztañaga Baggen
Beverley Thornton
Nora Grace Martinez

*Events Coordinator*
Michael Howrie

*Financial Coordinator*
Julia Guillermina

*Workshop Coordinator*
Wren True

*Website Manager*
Juliann Guerra

*Outreach Officer*
Anna Jones

*Editors*
Alice Rogers
Tom Carroll
Hayley Bernier
Lola Gaztañaga Baggen
Miriam Huxley
Tess Simpson
Anthi Cheimariou
Alyssa Osiecki
Anna Jones
Katie Hay-Molopo
Michael Howrie
Nicole Christine Caratas
Hanna-Maria Vester
Elena Sims

# FOREWORD

Here we are, in our second volume, in our second year. I am delighted to share this latest volume of *Hillfire Anthology* with you. It contains a great variety of short stories and poems (and some writings in between), all of which are published here for the first time. This book was made by a fantastic team, so my first big THANK YOU goes to you, team, for making this happen with me. It has been a joy – let's do it again!

My second big THANK YOU goes to those who have bought this book and supported our writing community here at Hillfire Press. Your support means that we can keep doing what we love to do, bringing new writing into the world.

The Hillfire journey started in Edinburgh, where many of us met during our various creative writing degrees. Since then, writers from further afield have joined us, and our community is growing. At Hillfire, we're aiming to keep the joy in writing alive, and keep the focus on the process – on creating and sharing the work. The pieces in this anthology have been workshopped and edited multiple times by fellow writers in the anthology. Thank you, writers, for supporting each other and trusting Hillfire with your work.

When I was looking for a name for this press, I thought about Arthur's Seat, the iconic hill in Edinburgh's Holyrood Park, which is covered in gorse. In spring, the bright yellow flowers light up the whole hillside so bright you can see it from miles away. I love how these small flowers can create such a spectacular effect together. This is what I'm aiming for with Hillfire: to collect pieces of writing that burn even brighter in combination. I am very excited to announce that since publishing Volume One, we have teamed up with The Selkie, a literary magazine championing underrepresented voices. If you like our work, look out for their publications, too!

In the last four years, I have edited two anthologies, and in the forewords to each of them, I wrote that 'we have made this book during a very challenging time,' hoping that the next one would be easier, the times less challenging. But writing the foreword to this volume, I'm tempted to write the same thing again. The challenges are here to stay. Democracies are fragile. Our rights to strike and protest have been threatened here in the UK and globally. Strikes and protests are tools with which many of our human rights have been won, and an attack on them is an attack on our human rights. We have also seen people come together to defend these rights, and our future, creating hope. This continues to be our shared responsibility. Art is political, life is political; the way we do things is political. This is no time to 'keep politics out of it'.

While we're doing this work, it is essential to rest and take care of ourselves and each other. Art can both be food for thought and welcome escape. I hope you find some of both in these pages.

Thank you, again, for supporting us by buying a copy of our anthology. I hope you enjoy it!

*Lena Kraus*
*Editor-in-Chief*

## A NOTE ON THIS BOOK

This is an anthology produced by writers from all over the world, which is reflected in different varieties of English.

We have included content identifiers in the table of contents, much like allergens on a menu, so that if there are topics you don't want to read about, we have hopefully provided you with a means to avoid them.

# CONTENTS

## CONTENT IDENTIFIERS

Death * Loss † Sexual assault ‡

Gore § Abusive relationships ¶ Drug use ‖

Suicide # Self-harm △ Domestic violence ◊

Human trafficking ∞ Objectification ø

## ZALA JAMBROVIC HATIC

*One Great Dane, Please*

Walking out of the Housing Department, I glanced at my watch and muttered a curse. I'd planned to be out of here hours ago. The muscles of my neck and shoulders were sore and I was exhausted, but I still had to deal with the curveball the Vetting Board had thrown at me.

What to do, what to do? Moving away from the door and out of the torrent of people flooding in and out of the department, I sacrificed a few moments to activate the personal comms unit implanted just under the skin of my left forearm. I pulled up one of the countless chat rooms dedicated to analyzing the VB's assessments and scrolled through the topics, searching for solutions to *stagnant assessment*. It had taken me three vetting cycles to save up enough to afford the new condo, and the board had taken one look at my file earlier that day and determined my existence was "personally and professionally unfulfilling and quickly becoming stagnant."

With my hereafter projection on the line, that was *not* a label I wanted to have on my record. Unfortunately, it appeared this was one of the more difficult tags to shake.

Around me, the underbelly of the Galleria was crawling with people fresh from the VB. Department reps circled them like sharks, trying to sell them everything from accommodations to instant education to health improvements.

I rubbed my eyes. A dull prodding ache had developed behind them sometime between my fifth and sixth hour in the Galleria. Even with a rock-solid plan, it had taken me almost all day to make it through the numerous departments of the boisterous, chaotic motley of showrooms and booths.

With a groan of frustration, I made a beeline for the PetDep. As soon as I crossed the showroom threshold, a rep materialized out of thin air, sporting a friendly grin and oozing eagerness.

"Welcome to the Pet Department of the Galleria, where dreams come to life!"

*Only for those who can afford them,* I thought, forcing my lips into a semblance of a smile. A friendly attitude made it easier to negotiate a better deal, and I would need a good price to afford this unexpected purchase.

"I would like to acquire a pet, please," I said, following the rep to an empty cocktail table.

"Certainly, sir! Would this be a live pet, or are you looking to upgrade your hereafter projection?" the rep said, fingers flying over the screen of the tablet in his hand. My personal comms unit pinged with an incoming connection request, and I approved it, giving the rep access to my profile.

"A live pet," I said. "I need to score better at my next appointment with the board."

The rep winced as he scrolled through my profile. "Hmm, I see."

The wince felt like a kick in the balls. I knew what the tablet would tell him—mid-thirties; commonplace education; lack of notable achievements, professional or otherwise; and a point sum trapped somewhere between scant and pitiful after my expensive stop at the HouseDep. I needed to spice things up, and quickly. If I didn't score better on my next assessment, I would be in real danger of having my hereafter projection scrapped, and I wasn't ready to give up the afterlife I'd spent my whole life carefully designing.

"What kind of pet would you like?" the rep asked with a bright smile. "Foxes are all the rage lately, wallabies too. Or perhaps something smaller, like an axolotl."

"Nothing exotic," I said before he could barrel on with his wild suggestions. The last thing I wanted was to spend a ridiculous amount of time learning how to care for an animal I knew nothing about. "Maybe a cat."

The rep gave me a sympathetic smile. "With all due respect, sir, I don't think a cat is the right choice. They are far too independent. You need an animal that will require more attention, something that will convince the board you've formed a bond and therefore  progressed emotionally, enriching your spirit. If you really don't want to consider anything exotic, the most traditional and suitable option would be a dog."

A life-size hologram of a Great Dane appeared on the small platform next to the table and I flinched. "Don't you have anything smaller?"

The rep glanced at my profile. "You have the space for it, sir. Great Danes do just fine in apartments as long as they are cared for properly."

As I watched, the animal shook its head, spit flying everywhere from its sagging jowls.

"You need something that will make you stand out," the rep said, skimming over my life as if it were a neatly arranged charcuterie board, just waiting to be plucked and picked at. "If the VB deems your existence mediocre again at your next assessment, your hereafter projection will get scrapped." His voice dropped to a whisper at the end, and he glanced around to make sure no one overheard his distressing statement.

I sighed, running my fingers through my hair for the two dozenth time that day.

"Dogs are very cliché pets," he went on, "so if you don't want anything more exotic, it is imperative you select a striking breed. Ideally, you'd want a rare breed such as a Lundehund or a Foxhound, but I'm afraid you don't have a sufficiently high score to afford those." He gave an awkward smile. "Which leaves you with a visually striking breed."

The Dane-hologram stretched, drawing attention to its massive size. I imagined it in my new condo, running around and knocking things over, shedding all over the place. I didn't want a dog. I didn't want a pet. But *something* had to change.

In an ideal world, I would focus my efforts on professional growth, but my current possibility of career advancement was close to zero, and I didn't know if I would find a suitable new position with a brighter future before my next assessment. Since accessing the Galleria was only possible directly after an appointment with the VB, leaving without a pet today carried too much risk.

And relationships …

While entering a coital relationship with someone would certainly indicate personal and emotional growth, people were so hideously flawed that the thought itself was repulsive. No, a relationship of any sort would remain off the table until my score was good enough to acquire a Partner.

I glanced at the RomDep just barely visible beyond the grand fountain that occupied the center of the indoor plaza at the heart of the Galleria. The dog, even if I managed to get a good deal, would set me back, further postponing my visit to the department.

"Danes aren't too expensive, either," the rep droned on, oblivious to my internal turmoil, "so you can afford it with your current score, along with some upgrades. One of our most popular extras is the Anti-Motion-Sickness add-on. It only costs an extra 50 points, and—" he gave a laugh "—trust me, it makes life a lot easier, especially with a breed like the Great Dane. Big dogs produce a lot of puke, so the AMS is definitely a good idea for anyone with a pod. Another popular add-on is Increased Cuddling Tendencies, with the option to select the degree on a scale of one to ten, and then there is also …"

Twenty minutes later, I left the PetDep holding the leash of a harlequin Great Dane after convincing the rep I only wanted the standard Starter's Package with no add-ons apart from built-in house training. He hadn't been happy, but I wasn't about to spend more than absolutely necessary on this, and I'd put my foot down.

The Dane trotted next to me, his long legs easily keeping pace with my quick stride as we headed toward the exit. Notorious for being the slowest and busiest department, RomDep had a line of people winding from its door around the entire indoor plaza like a snake, and I muttered apologies as I squeezed between two people queuing. The Dane did his best to sniff both of them and shove his big head where it didn't belong, which had me muttering additional apologies. The woman smiled and gave the dog a quick pet. The man leveled a death glare at the wet spot on his leg, courtesy of the Dane's drooling, before telling me to piss off.

It was understandable, really. He'd probably been waiting for hours, and he wasn't even close to the door. Acquiring a Partner was *expensive*, so when you finally built up a good enough score to afford one, you wanted to make sure they came with *just* the right nose and *just* the right IQ and *just* the right amount of daddy issues. The reps didn't help matters any. They frequently spent hours convincing a client that four orgasms per intercourse really was worth the extra 450 points, or that an upgrade of the Partner's sense of humor would help decrease the client's stress levels in the afterlife.

When the time finally came, my own trip to RomDep would be quick as a wink. Countless hours of fantasizing had left me with such a clear-cut image of my desired Partner, I could draw their portrait. I knew their every feature, personality trait, and quirk. When I could finally afford to acquire a Partner, I knew exactly what I would choose: Egyptian feet, a crooked smile, British accent. I would acquire them for my hereafter projection, of course—only fools and those with whopping scores got a live one. Why waste a Partner on however many cycles remained to you on this plane of existence when you could get them for eternity in the afterlife?

Something wet touched my hand and I looked down to see the Dane licking my knuckles. He looked up at me with big brown eyes and cocked his head to the side, as if asking me why we'd stopped.

I wiped my hand on my trousers and turned my back on the RomDep. One day, I'd get there, and my hereafter would be worth anything I had to sacrifice until then.

TODD WORKMAN

*To an Autumn Eve*

"Season of mists and mellow fruitfulness,
    Close bosom-friend of the maturing sun…"

– John Keats


Rest and commune
        with ripened rays, sip
                the mellow twilight,

bid it dusk you in settling blue
        as sylvan mists hold
                a breath.

WENDELIN LAW

*Plunder, Hearts, Plundered*
*—ten tankas; Edinburgh, September 2022*

### 1

brown paper, lost ink
the old receipt clasped within
a loved vintage book
—to whom else shall I confess
how these rouge nights ravish me

### 2

*—why?* I asked and asked
till words confined existence
existence, gorge, words—
hot-red mouthfuls—trickling down
—down my lips flaring *why, why—*

### 3

leaves, *komorebi*
gravitate to woodland paths
rock-stars, toe-taps, mulch
sing—*when in forests, one could
only think of oneself dead*

4

under Arthur's Seat
desiccated wings whir and
plunder hearts—plundered
hard—snuffed minds fluttered in wind
—away—in wind—
                    throb—and drop


5

dropped wings dropped, in vain
I—lost to dawning darkness
saw strayed eyes strayed, slain
defeated by senseless wars
breathless, lying—I am bare


6

in festoons they hang
there's no hay in Haymarket
trash hangs, trash pours, trash
up and beyond Dalry's fields
not of wheat, but concrete shits


7

praise the arcane moon
you are steadfast, beautiful
we name you the Queen
white, undying, but lying
in state, forever, the Queen

### 8

*O, God save the Queen*
said drunk men in drunken pants
—two wet patches drew
a map. To all things fallen—
pints raised—cheers to the air (heir)

### 9

cortège long cortège
crowds come, crowds go, crowds protest
catch a glimpse to brag
For what do your jewels flash?
Glints of blood-sweat: *hip, hooray!*

### 10

conceive by my light
thorough, thorough, thoroughly
darling, you are fucked
by the venereal Sun
that never sets, never rests

### *Coda*

incorrigible
nights soaked in blood-red, they come
surreptitiously.
again—Sun still glaring, but
lo, the people are undressed

JULIANN GUERRA

*Puppy Love*

"What did you do?" Madeline demanded as soon as the call connected.

"Hello, my dear friend," replied Kenzie, in a tone very much like a mother asking a toddler to say *please* before handing over a toy the child was begging for. "I miss you. I know we texted earlier today, but I haven't heard your voice since yesterday."

Madeline started strumming her fingers on the counter in front of her.

"That's how you start a conversation," Kenzie educated her. "With as many as we've had, I'm a bit surprised I have to remind you."

"What did you do?" Madeline repeated, rolling her eyes so hard she was surprised Kenzie didn't make a comment, even though she couldn't see the action through the phone.

"What did I do? As in: how was my day?" Kenzie asked. "It was fine. Went to the store for some final touches to decorate with."

Madeline knew *final touches* could range from a few new plants to enough removable wallpaper to cover the entire apartment. She made a mental note to check in next week to see if Kenzie was brave enough to actually decorate. Kenzie had met her new roommate online and confided in Madeline about how she couldn't tell if the girl liked her or not. They were very different, and Kenzie was nervous her roommate would be unimpressed by her interior decorating skills. So far she had just been purchasing the decorations and shoving them into the corner of her bedroom.

"As nice as that sounds," Madeline said. "I meant what I originally asked."

"Okay, I give up. What are you talking about?"

"*Puppy Love.*"

"*Puppy ...*" Kenzie started to ask for clarification before letting out a laugh. "Oh my god! They picked you?"

"Yes," Madeline said curtly. "I came home today to a very large manila envelope with a contract and welcome packet. It was like being accepted into college all over again. Except I didn't apply to *Puppy Love.*"

"I can't believe they picked you." Kenzie's laughs were coming in strong through the phone.

"Hey!" Madeline couldn't help but let a slight sense of hurt color her response.

"No, not like that. You're a perfect candidate for *Puppy Love.* I just mean that those have to be crazy odds."

"According to this pamphlet, my application was one of twenty, chosen from hundreds. *Hundreds*, Kenzie. That's not a lot. That's less than a thousand because if they had over a thousand applicants, they would have said that."

"Don't downgrade it; I worked hard on that application."

"But why?" Madeline asked with an exasperated laugh. It was difficult not to find the idea of Kenzie giggling to herself as she made up an application the tiniest bit funny.

"Because you bought Callisto during quarantine, and I saw an ad for casting on Instagram."

As if knowing she was being talked about, Madeline's year-and-a-half-old pit bull sauntered into the room, slid her front paws forward to stretch her back, and gave a big yawn before sitting in front of Madeline with expectant eyes. Madeline scratched between her ears.

"I bought a puppy, so that means I want to be on a dating show? Are pit bulls even allowed?"

Callisto's head tilted to the side curiously.

"No idea."

"Did you even read this description? It sounds like animal and human abuse to me."

"I did. But I will admit that a bottle of wine was also involved, so some details may have slipped through the cracks."

Madeline cleared her throat dramatically before picking up one of the pieces of paper from the manilla envelope.

"'*Puppy Love* is the newest take on a reality dating show coming to streaming services next fall,'" she read in her best news anchor voice. "'While similar shows may involve flowers, personality tests, or blind dates, *Puppy Love* has something even better: puppies! Every contestant comes onto the set of *Puppy Love* as a single dog parent in search of the perfect human/dog combination to complete their family. Will contestants who already have so much love for their pets be able to open their hearts to another ... and a human?'"

"I can already see the drama unfolding," Kenzie said excitedly. "The dogs love each other, but the humans can't stand each other. A chihuahua pees all over the house, even though its owner swears it's house-trained. Why wouldn't you want to be a part of this?"

"I'm not doing this." Madeline shook her head at Callisto, who smiled. Madeline took that as agreement. Being stuck with strangers for weeks on end sounded like her worst nightmare. She could never imagine putting her dog through that.

"Honestly, I'm surprised it took this long for one of your applications to be chosen," Kenzie continued.

"One of my applications?" Madeline snapped back to attention. "What does that mean?"

"All throughout senior year I sent in applications for you to almost every dating show I could think of. Why do you think I was always asking you questions when we were watching TV?"

"That's what you were doing?" Madeline demanded. Callisto, who had laid down, picked her head up.

Kenzie's random Would You Rather questions about house types and which celebrities Madeline and her other roommates would date always came off as fun questions to get through commercial breaks. Not so much anymore.

"Don't act so shocked. You signed me up for FarmersOnly freshman year. I still get emails sometimes."

"I stand by that. I think you'd be happy with a cowboy type."

"And I think you'd be happy with a man who has a dog." Kenzie's tone was accusatory, shocked by Madeline's hypocrisy. "It's the same thing."

"Signing someone up for a website and getting someone cast on a reality TV show are two very different things."

"You should at least consider it."

"Why?"

"Because it could be fun! You probably won't fall in

love, but you might meet some cool people. And I know job hunting during the pandemic has been tough, but this experience could make you famous enough to be the face of some type of collagen pill. The income from that alone should have you packing a suitcase."

Madeline let out a laugh. Just when she thought Kenzie was going to say something inspirational, she hits her with the exciting prospect of paid social media posts.

"I'm glad you have manageable expectations for me."

"It will also give me something to watch while I'm stuck out here in Indiana," Kenzie added wistfully. "Think of all the people who would want to be my friend when I turn on *Puppy Love* and point you out as my best friend."

"You're in grad school at the University of Notre Dame. I don't feel bad for you."

The conversation shifted to Kenzie talking about her classes and the restaurants she was hoping to try in her new neighborhood. Eventually, Callisto's pleading eyes were too much to ignore, and Madeline started wrapping up the conversation.

"Don't you dare throw out that *Puppy Love* offer without at least considering stepping out of your comfort zone," Kenzie warned. Madeline felt an imaginary finger pointing right at her face.

"You should talk," she accused. "You're afraid to hang up a picture because it might not match your roommate's *vibe*."

"I'll face my fear if you face yours."

"Goodbye, Kenzie."

"Sure, she can't say hello, but she has no issue saying goodbye," Kenzie mumbled through the receiver.

"Love you."

"Love you, too. I'll talk to you later."

Madeline started cleaning up the mail that was covering her desk. She gathered the *Puppy Love* information and walked to the recycling bin, ready to get rid of it. She paused just as she was about to throw it in the bin. Madeline looked over to Callisto standing by the door, eager for a walk.

"What do you think, Calli? Should we give it a try?"

ELENA SIMS

*Devil in the Dark*

You're alone on the street when you see him.

It's dark, night has long since come, and you silently curse that you let the time get away from you, let your girlfriends slide one more drink your way in the pub. They Ubered home, but you, you live close enough to walk. So you do. Briskly.

Brisk is the only pace when the sun goes down.

You pass a streetlamp and then a noisy pub. This brings you comfort. You can hide in the noise, blend yourself in with the brunette girl puking on the curb, her friend on the phone behind her. This is how you were raised to walk.

From sanctuary to sanctuary like hopscotch.

You pass the girls somewhat reluctantly. Something has felt off since you waved goodbye to your friends. A shadow in your peripheral. A figure too far away to know if it is there. Not enough evidence for immediate alarm, but enough to make you pull out your dead cell phone and stick it to your ear. You curse yourself again, for letting the battery run out before the day did.

The road ahead is dark. The streetlights have gone off, like they do sometimes. Ghosts, your friends often joke. Edinburgh has a history, after all. And even though you don't believe it, your heart quickens. The familiar friend of urgency guiding you across the street for no other reason than your gut says so.

And then, he is there.

Not a ghost, but a tall silhouette lagging behind on the side of the pavement you just walked away from. A man in grey joggers and a black sweatshirt. For the next few moments, you're glad you crossed the road as you both walk a safe distance on parallel pavements.

But then, he crosses the street.

Small dread sets in, your legs itchy and hot as they hasten. You feign laughter into the cold silence of your phone and reassure yourself this guy is just going home. That he probably doesn't even realise he's making you uncomfortable. Like that night those boys followed too closely behind as they struggled to carry their drunk mate home. Or when the old man chased you down the block only to ask directions.

This too, you think, is most likely the same.

He says nothing to you but continues along a few feet behind.

First down one street, then two. Then four.

The only sounds in the night are the thumping of determined shoes smacking against the pavement. Your heels click faster. His trainers accommodate. Your breath deepens. You are trying to keep up the talking, the mindless chatter. But he's gotten even closer, only a few steps between now. And suddenly it feels like he knows you're faking the call, feels like he's been paying attention. And you wonder, growing more afraid by the minute, if he's been there since you waved goodbye to your friends.

From the first shadow you glanced over your shoulder.

And it doesn't matter if he's just going home anymore.

It doesn't matter if you're overthinking it all. You cannot help it.

You begin to run.

And then, so does he.

Only months ago, the Met Police released a statement. The guidelines simple. Be louder. Be faster. Wave down a bus.

But your voice is a whisper. Your legs quiver as they go. There are no buses on the street. And even if there were, those assholes don't stop for anyone.

So instead, you run until your breath cannot keep up. Your legs burn. Your stomach lurches. He's right behind you. This isn't a drill. This isn't like those last times.

This can't be happening.

But the truth is, it surely can. And it is.

Suddenly, his fingers are on your wrist, and you're yanked to a stop. Suddenly, your voice catches on the wind and the words are ripped from your lungs.

'Let go!' you scream, a ragged, shrill sound.

But instead of release, another hand finds your waist and now you are struggling together. Like threads of yarn yanking and twisting and tangling around each other. You don't know when your phone left your grip, but your fingers are free and sharp. Without a thought, you slash nails into flesh, hearing the grunt of an angered man.

There is a hard knock on your forehead, and you tumble to the ground. Your vision blurs, and you cry. Willing yourself to stay awake. Afraid of what will happen without yourself present. But your eyes close anyway.

Darkness swarms.

Before your story continues, here is a little about him.

He was raised in an average family, although it hardly matters.

Growing up, he saw how his mother cooked dinner while his father watched television each night. How his secondary school friends hooted at every girl who passed them on the pavement. How his younger sisters were scolded for their low-cut tops, their too-short skirts. And he agreed, of course. With those clothes, they would give a man the wrong impression one day.

One day, they would be asking for it.

Once, in uni, a friend of his confided that she had been molested by an older man on the bus. The very night after the incident, she claimed that although not every man was a rapist, almost every rapist was just an ordinary man.

To which he quickly replied, 'Nonsense, generalisations like that are ignorant.'

Rapists were cut from a different cloth. After all, he was an ordinary man and he was definitely *not* a rapist. Clearly, he decided, she must be exaggerating.

And to be honest, she had always been a little too innocent. Maybe the incident on the bus had been a misunderstanding on her part. Maybe the older gentleman hadn't meant anything by it. Maybe she had just taken it out of context like women did sometimes.

After all, she was a little ugly.

But you.

You are beautiful, he thinks when he sees you in the pub tonight.

He finds your thick black jumper alluring. The curve of your jeans inviting. You haven't looked his way once, but he's had a few drinks and knows you're just playing hard to get. You go outside and he follows, watching as you wave goodbye to your friends.

He knows you've been drinking too. That for both of you, tonight is all about harmless fun. After all, he knows girls only get drunk for attention.

And then you begin to walk, and so does he, noting how the streetlights have gone out ahead.

You open your eyes again.

You did not faint, although you came close. You feel as if your body and mind separated and only now are you recombining, regaining control.

Beside you, he lies motionless on the ground.

One of your heels is somehow in your palm, the black stiletto slick with a wet that smears across your fingers, violent and red. You almost begin to cry, but a cold gust of air shushes you. Someone else is there.

A pair of copper eyes greet you, the girl's red hair blazing in the night as she smiles. And even though you've never met or even heard of her before, her identity comes to you in waves, like an old song remembered.

Geillis Duncan, last witch to burn in Edinburgh.

A witch, because her herbal remedies healed the sick too well.

A witch, because a woman of devilry is more believable than a woman of science.

They twisted metal pins under her nails just to hear her scream. Claimed her the Devil's child until they had her almost believing it. Raked their hands up and down until her flesh was raw, her body all used up.

What little was left, she used to curse the man who saw her dancing on the beach that night. A girl who had only wanted to feel the moonlight on her back. The sand beneath her feet. She cursed them as they raped her. As they goaded her in her cell. As they stacked the kindling high and lit the flame.

You desperately wonder *why* they did this.

More than four hundred years later, the answer hasn't changed.

*Because they can.*


And then there is this man, dead on the street before you.

You look at your hand, and the bloodied heel.

'Did I kill him?' you ask Geillis.

'We did,' she states.

You drop the shoe. It tumbles onto his back, and then the grass.

Geillis smiles.

She whispers:

*Good job,* to you.

*Good riddance,* to him.

And then she is gone, and so are you.

Like a spell onto the night, you are back in front of the pub, waving off your friends. They clamber into a back seat, and for a moment you debate scooting in too. Debate whisking off with them into the night, or even just into the safety of the car's heater. But you don't do it. After all, you live close enough to walk.

You look out, towards the dark streets ahead. Unaware he is watching you, even in this moment. But rest assured, as you pass a noisy pub, she too is with you in the dark.

Two copper pennies keeping watch.

MICHAEL HOWRIE

*His Hedge*

He – let's call him 'he' – walks down the steps to his garden and takes in the view. Ratty, overgrown, half-scorched and half-overwatered, his paradise is enclosed on all sides. Behind him is the irregular stone of the house, to the sides are the tall wooden fences which obscure all views of his neighbours and to the end of the garden is the dense, dark web of his hedge.

The hedge has never really caught his eye before. But something sets it off this evening, something about the weak light that hangs between dusk and sunset. For all his years in the house, he has never properly considered the hedge. It's like the plain cornicing of a room, the margins of a sheet of paper, the never-cleaned backside of a tap. But now the hedge looms large in his vision, its countless leaves thrumming tonelessly through his mind, and he is drawn to the end of the garden to inspect it closer. Standing next to the branches and leaves dulls some of the strange fascination, but his determination remains. He knows he must part the foliage with his hands, crouch on the dewy ground and push his head in for a look.

'Come on, back to the nest,' a blackbird calls.

He – our 'he' – furrows his brows. The bird appears to be talking to a second, smaller bird.

'That's it, get in, little one. And take that thing off your neck.'

'I don't see why I should have to take it off,' the blackbird chick complains. It's wearing the yellow ring of a drinks bottle around its neck. 'It looks good on me.'

'It looks ridiculous,' the large blackbird responds. This must be the parent, he thinks: must be the father with its jet-black plumage and stern, yellow beak.

The chick shakes the ring off and makes a motion as if to throw it deep into the hedge – but obviously and clumsily tucks the yellow bit of plastic behind the nest instead.

'You're not the smartest of my children, are you?'

The chick sheepishly begs its case. 'Just this one? Can't I keep one?'

'So you can catch on a branch and snap your neck? Or an owl take its claws to your throat? You know the story of your brother and the netting.'

'No I don't. What brother?'

'Exactly. And your future siblings won't know what happened to you either if you don't rid yourself of that rubbish.'

The chick's current siblings appear from the gloom, stumbling their grey bodies towards the nest. The line of fuzz, however, is not uniform. Some of the chicks have tied bright threads around their legs. Others have draped wrappers around their necks, while others still have clipped bread bag tabs to their wings. As each of them clambers into the nest, the blackbird father's beak clacks open like a gawping marionette. At the end of the line, another bird appears, an almost tawny thrush, which he – our he – assumes must be the mother. The parents share a glance as if to ask, 'What can we do?'

Our he finally takes his head out from the hedge but maintains his awkward crouch. Overwhelmed by the oddness, he's been holding his head for too long under unfathomable waters. He is not a fanciful man. He was never the most imaginative of fathers, never the one to play make-believe or indulge in childish games. The last he saw them, his children still held this fault against him, and he doesn't know exactly how to proceed. Now, snapped out of the lulling dream of the feeling that had brought him to the hedge, he has to act rather than follow. Acting has not been tailored into his strong suit for some time, and so he stays for a while, crouching in front of the hedge in a mardy dither, not wanting to choose between the comfort of mundanity and the terrible excitement of a hedge of birds.

'They're a nest of failures,' the blackbird father scoffs.

'They can hear us,' replies the mother.

'Dead within a week, every last one of them, I'm telling you.'

The nest is full of chicks, bodies crammed against one another and accessories on show. The first chick has returned the yellow ring to its neck and smugly placed itself in the centre of the nest.

'I think we'll survive,' the first chick chimes in. The blackbird parents swing their beaks sideways to fix an eye each on their child. 'We just need to be careful.' The rest of the nest bob their heads, flaunting their regalia and squeaking in approval.

'I'm not having it. We've seen enough young birds wasting away with nothing but rubbish in their gullet. It's like you're all begging for the grave,' says the mother.

'We won't eat the stuff! It's just to wear, just for us.'

'I'm sorry. I'm sorry I didn't keep things tidier.' The birds fix their beady eyes on the man. His speech surprises him and our he freezes to the spot. After no more than a second of pause, they're all gone. The nest is nowhere to be seen, and a tiredness washes over him. A regret at having intruded on the moment exhausts his bones, and he finds his way back up the garden and into his home.

Slumped in a tall-backed armchair at the side of his kitchen-cum-living room, he notices he left the back door open. An evening chill blows in, and he sees that the light is truly fading. He's sad to have disturbed the birds, and even sadder to think he might have caused them harm. He supposed if he was going to call it 'his' hedge, he had a responsibility to keep it clean. But over the past few years he'd let all responsibility slip through his fingers.

Before he can dwell too heavily on his own pity, a bird flaps down to the back door of the kitchen. It seems to think for a moment before crossing the portal. Immediately, a second bird appears, alighting on a counter. They're blackbirds, but he's unable to tell if they're his same ones. When a third appears, a fourth soon follows, then a fifth and a sixth.

The birds keep flying in, more and more of them taking perch on the kitchen cabinets, roosting in every spare bowl, cramming the rafters with yellow, black and brown beaks and feathers. It reminds him of years back when the children lived in the house with him, when he was overrun with absurdly small hands and footprints, and there was never an unpunctuated moment of calm. In the chaos of wings and blackbirds, he can't remember where his own children have all gone; when was the last time anyone called? They used to drop by, use the spare key, let themselves in unannounced. But now they've become strange, controlled by the whims of an unknown impulse, thrown off the shackles of their parents and never think to visit our he.

The birds begin to clothe themselves. Loose papers and unwanted letters he's left on the countertops become crumpled jackets and folded hats. The curtains are pecked into flowy shirts and long scarves. All he can do is sit back and watch. Some inkling of frustration sits in a node of his chest, but it's dwarfed by an uncontrollable, warm and numbing joy. He sinks deeper into the chair and his arms and legs grow still, still enough for the birds to begin to perch on him too.

While at first it seems as though the birds don't notice him, over time they tentatively drape scraps of frayed curtain and unwashed socks from the laundry on his arms and shoulders. Progressively, the draping reaches his feet until only his head is left uncovered. The birds continue to flock inside, the house becoming a throb of black and brown and grey, punctuated with splashes of bright accents: phonebook pages turned into tiny gloves, fridge magnets made into scaled cloaks and the occasional flash of gold from miniscule chocolate wrapper shoes.

Our he feels himself slide deeper into the chair, falling into the depths of the feathered mass until he slips, inescapably, out and into the throng. Finally free, he glides weightlessly through the fluttering blackness and starts to pull out wrappers from the bin, sticking them together into the beginnings of a cloak.

SKYE WILSON

*Are we there yet?*

The sun spills
through my car
windows, this car
that feels like truly
mine, like strong tea
and long lunches.
With my shining pink
driving licence
pulsing in my purse,
I steer, eyes alert and
laughing as you crack
a can, feed me joyous
chocolate buttons.
We use our silliest
voices for songs
we're not sure
why we love, except
they make us feel
like sides of
mountains, like
the luck
of unsplatted
insects, like
the skeleton
of a leaf stuck
to a bird's foot,
like flying,
despite our bags
weighing us down.

SKYE WILSON

*Where I grew up, a burn is a river*


A stranger's gaze, gone
before I catch it, haunts.

*Skinned knees and the heather
of my first kiss. Drunken lights,
notebooks filled with love letters
and unintelligible lists.*

A plunging face of rock
sprouts from a shallow
that ripples like a thousand
wrinkled fingertips.

*A singing, scraping ache
of throat, frayed rope swing
in my fingers, gasp
and slap in freezing burn,
feet made clean and cold.*

I catch my own eye
in a mirror-dark moment
of still water, reach
towards the blurred face,
clutch with unfamiliar
fingers, burn.

*Origins*

For one day, I met a girl with gappy teeth
and a birthmark just like mine. My frozen fingers
spluttered to a start, all careful lettering
and longing—I wrote *Sophie Sophie Sophie*
until I ran out of pages and that diary slipped
to the back of a drawer. My first real poem,
full of exclamation marks and awkward line breaks,

was about our croft: the sharp sting of nettles;
the salt smack of the loch below; mud-caked
boots and the neighbour's daughter.
My dad hung it on his office wall and I,
too, was hooked—falling in love again,
again, again, writing poems for each new
adoration, becoming more myself with every word.

ALEXANDRA YE

*To the Pagoda*

I want so badly for Liza to love me. Liza, who is so tall and successful and complete, how can I help it? She won't look at me, but suddenly her babysitter has fallen through today. Is there any chance I can step in? I want to ask her where she's going, whether it's some kind of date, and can I come, but instead I immediately accept. If Liza won't love me, at least I can get her daughter on my side.

I meet Noemie just as her mother is leaving, sweeping out the door in a long summer dress. I resist the urge to reach for Liza's skirt with my fingertips. Instead, once she is gone, I tell Noemie: We are taking a trip to the mall. She looks at me dubiously. She is one of those organic children, raised on analog entertainment and steamed vegetables. She has never been to the mall, she tells me, confirming what I have long suspected—that her whole life has been portioned into enrichment activities, like watercolor painting and breathwork for emotional self-regulation, and no, she's never needed to hop around a mall like some little consumerist animal. Liza would hate this kind of trip; it's like I am committing a form of sabotage. Still, I am triumphant. My plan is a brilliant plan. I know precisely what will get Noemie to like me: baby's first cinnamon roll. I buckle her into the back of my car, the seat belt loose.

I have a booster seat, usually, she says, and I tell her, this is a fun special trip where you get to sit in the big seat, like a grown-up.

She is unimpressed.

I drive to the very top of the parking garage and she continues to look sour. We walk through the department stores, I spray the fancy perfumes, she makes an ugly face and says it smells like garbage. O, Noemie, she is so small and so baleful and mean, so unmoved by the maniacal thrashing of the bubble tea shaking machines.

You can have whatever you want, I say, in another effort to indulge her, but she just gives me a look as if I certainly could not afford it. We drift away from the extensive menu of bubble tea toppings and meander fruitlessly through the food court. But she doesn't want anything. Not the uncannily aromatic cinnamon rolls, not the pretzels, not the iced strawberry frappes. She doesn't feel like trying on dresses, she doesn't like to play juvenile games. She is mortified when I grasp the joystick controlling the claw machine, walking straight past before I even put any money in. Inside the plastic box, the stuffed toys are piled into a mute little heap, so dejected, so acutely flammable. She doesn't like the unicorns or the sparkly blue owls or the sticky soccer balls; the claw hangs there, flaccid, and the change in my pocket starts feeling cheap.

We walk countless loops around the stores and I drag her up some downward escalators, which only embarrasses her. This is fine, I think, she'll be delighted eventually, but at the same time I worry that Liza is right, children need enrichment activities, and I, in fact, have holes in my brain from having spent so much time lurking in malls as a child, trailing behind my sister and her friends, eating samples of weirdly astringent orange chicken, watching the other children throw tantrums and bruise their knees on the cold beige marble floors while their mothers stand beside them in horror. Noemie is already a different species of person. She already knows more about the world than me.

Soon we have walked the entire mall, and we end up standing at one of the glass railings, looking down at the wishing fountain below. It's a cloudy day outside and the light in the mall is blank and gray, the pennies in the fountain dull, flat, inert. I take the change out of my pocket and contemplate wishing for Liza to love me.

You make a wish for something too, I tell Noemie. You must want something.

Noemie takes the penny from me, but she's distracted. Something has finally caught her eye. I prod her again: What do you want, Noemie?

It takes her a long time to respond, but when her answer comes, it's decisive. I want to go there, Noemie says. I want to get my ears pierced. She points at the kiosk behind me, its luminous display of cheap, glittering earrings. A tall, anemic teenager is perched on a stool in the middle of it all, scrolling on his phone.

Dread washes over me. You cannot get your ears pierced, I tell Noemie. You cannot do that unless your mother allows it.

She frowns. Her ears look formless and squishy but perfect, like gnocchi. It's not fair, she says. All of my cousins' ears are pierced. You said I could have anything I wanted. You promised.

I watch as the teenaged piercing salesman tucks his hair behind his ear. I promised you could have any flavor of bubble tea you wanted, I correct her, but then she tells me: My mother says good people always keep their promises, and I think of Liza, who is so beautiful it makes me feel ashamed, Liza who lives in my dreams, Liza who only calls me when the babysitter falls through, and I feel my authority begin to slip.

It just really hurts, I say quickly, it hurts terribly, we are trying to protect you.

Noemie reaches up and pinches my left earlobe. Her fingers are small and hot. Is that why you don't have pierced ears either? Because it hurts too much?

No, I reply, I just don't want to.

She says: You don't want to be prettier? You don't want to be easier to love? She rolls and rolls my earlobe around between her fingers and suddenly I am remade, like clay, shrinking and shifting until I am not even an eight-year-old girl, like Noemie, or even a baby, or even a person, only the small blue polyester owl sitting atop the heap of toys in the claw machine that Noemie did not want to play with, worth twenty-five cents and a bit of luck. Noemie does not even need to pay, we owls just follow her around, desperate to please her, and so, in a matter of seconds, I am seated amidst the pagoda, my tiny stuffed wings folded in my lap, watching Noemie's gleeful eyes as the glumly rubber-gloved piercing technician raises his gun to my head.

WREN TRUE

*The Water Shawl*

You came to us a creature. Your skin was gray, and your
fingertips almost blue, almost translucent. Just a little
bird with paralyzed wings, and nothing to do except lie
back in the hands that cupped you, and look up at the
huge staring world. I remember thinking—knowing—
that we should have been identical. We should have
been the same child, with the same feelings. My image
of you was so different from the thing that was like a
crushed cicada's husk I saw being carried through our
saltwater house.

'It is a serious thing, sleep,' my father had said to me,
as we prepared for the arrival of the boy who had not
slept in nine years.

When I first heard of you, I didn't think it could be so
bad. If I never went to bed, I'd have more time to play.
This was a time when I couldn't imagine a more terrible
thing than skinning my knees, or catching my thumb in
the gate which led our sheep home.

'The Water Shawl will save him,' my father had said.
'Imagine. Staying up for nine years.'

I had thought that I very well could imagine it.

Your family traveled from far away to reach us, just to
lay you beneath the Water Shawl. Just to rest.

My family lives on steep slopes of green which give

way to the ocean. Our house smells like salt and our sheep move across the hills like noisy clouds. I was there, perched on the counter and looking through the window, when a mule-driven wagon tipped over the top of one of our hills, and jangled toward us. And that's when I first began to worry. I asked my father, what if the Water Shawl didn't work? What if it couldn't put you to sleep?

I don't remember the expression my father made. I imagine it was pensive, and perhaps his hands were propped on his hips, and the apron under his belly tied especially tight. I remember what he said, though: 'He will leave the way he came.'

And then what will happen? I asked my father.

'I'm not at all sure.'

So it was a serious thing.

We watched the clouds of our sheep part to allow your wagon to pass through, and then the sheep followed you all the way to the house, like a parade.

Your name is Fern. I watch over you, now, and your still brow. The way the hairs of your eyebrows stand. The way breath inflates your chest. You've honestly never looked better. But I remember when I first saw you.

There were many people in your family. We'd spent the day preparing food and making beds in the barn. The night of your arrival, our families ate together. It was a solemn business, which was disappointing. I wanted to meet you, show you my pet crickets and teach you how to coax a sheep into letting you ride it. There was something in my father's demeanor that told me to wait. Something about the long silences that crawled inside me and squeezed.

Your family was a reserved bunch. They apologized for everything and hardly ate the food themselves. When my father urged them to eat more, they did.

After the meal, my father pulled an old wooden crate across the floor, which had lacquered corners, and a latch that was broken. Inside lay the Water Shawl. It was—it *is*—a worn thing, and in desperate need of repair. The faded indigo rubs off on your fingertips like ash, and the embroidered stars which are dark, reddish brown, were once gold. My father was always terrified to mend it.

And then I saw you, Fern, for the first time. It was a beguiling thing to behold, you in someone's arms, carried into the bedroom we'd prepared for you. Limp and narrow and tiny and wide-eyed. Like an unblinking insect. Crusted eyelashes and chattering bones. A nameless weight had spread through our house and backed me into a wall—*so it was a serious thing*.

I was not familiar with that kind of dread—that sensation of hovering over a deep crevice or falling into the sea, the feeling that something bad might happen. Or that bad things happened to people sometimes, and here it was, hanging open like a yawning tomb, endless, swallowing but never catching you. Ah, this was it. This was what people were so afraid of. This was what made people tie their aprons too tight across their bellies. This was why the wagon jangled over the hill, why your family couldn't bear to eat. Ah, it was like waking up in the world. Drawing back from the threads and hairs I'd thought would always bind me, realizing I was alone. Or I could be, if I wasn't careful.

My final glimpse of you, before you were placed in a bed, before the Water Shawl was spread over you, over your face and your bug eyes, it was like you had died and we were saying goodbye. And I felt that whatever had been stifling me was torn, and I wept.

•

The Water Shawl was only supposed to put you to bed for one night. But the Shawl has been folded up and returned to its crate, and you've been here, sleeping, ever since. For twenty straight years.

That first night, our families celebrated. Old ladies hopped and did somersaults in the fields, and the children scream-sang funny songs into the night. Everybody got drunk and delirious and chased sheep. One person vanished and hasn't been seen since. That night, I celebrated cautiously. I picked wildflowers and brought them to you and put them in your hands as you slept. I talked to you while the singing and chanting of our families thrummed, blazed, caterwauled outside.

Now it's a little different. I put my own children under the Water Shawl when they won't go to bed, or the baby won't stop wailing. None of it bothers you. Nothing bothers you except when you're left alone. I think you get agitated. But I'm happy to tie flowers in your hair and rub dirt on your feet—you are a part of things, then. Endless, endless.

# HANNA-MARIA VESTER

## *Endometriosed*

Ancient infants idle
in situ on the uterine balcony
enjoying a smoke or four.

Legend has it, they rebel when you turn
thirty-two, stage
a sit-in-to-slide-out. Make a motherhood

maelstrom of your body and every
signifier you have left turns tiny
hands ever faster, dragging you, growing

you: ashtray, serving uproarious squall.
Revered screams mammaplasty reversed,
reduced to boob, banished to coop.

Diagnosed, endometriosed, mad
luck. I grow anti-yolk where fast hands can't tug.

HANNA-MARIA VESTER

*[Insert username] was on a bike ride*


You bike many miles,             in my emails

the notification every time you take another trip.

Sometimes I delete them. Sometimes

I let them sit there as memory

of something I was not part of.

But I can see you there

pedaling hard, sweating,   then     the

ease

of

the

slope

and

the

bend

at the end. Your hair too short

to note how deliciously the wind

befuddles you. Your face so red

from hitting the breeze.

Your softening pulse

whirling a waltz, as you stop, drinking

the view you made with your feet

dancing in circles. Dancing a way

on the map. I sharpen my binoculars,

adjusted to long-distance, zooming in –

I'm racing to wait for you

to be home

saved and sound.

ALEX PENLAND

*Finn*

Oh, this? It's apple divination. It's kind of a reflex, I guess? I've been doing it since I was a kid.

Yeah, so, in first grade, Mary Stalwart told me that if you say the alphabet while you twist off the stem of the apple, the letter it breaks off on is the first letter of your true love's name. I know it's stupid, but I do it every time. Like—here, see? A, B, C, D, E, F... There.

I mean, you remember how the playground works. Kids do all kinds of weird magic. Cootie catchers, yeah? Jump rope chants. And I was a weird one, so I took it way too seriously. Because, like, the premise doesn't make sense. You always get letters around the first half of the alphabet. Are people named Zachary or Zahra just doomed to a loveless existence? No one in the world has a soulmate named Zoe? If your name is April, can you, like, weaken the stems of your crush's apples and alter fate? And can you even imagine the breach of trust if you've been married for a decade or something and you come downstairs and find your husband Aaron madly worrying the stems of all your apples in case one day you get an M at lunch or something and start dating Marty in the next cubicle over?

(A, B, C, D, E, F... Ha! Two in a row!)

But, I mean, Mary Stalwart wouldn't have just *lied* to

me, so then I figured that, logically, the future could not possibly be set in stone. I decided that whatever I was doing between eating apples was changing my destiny. Like, maybe at snacktime my soulmate was some guy named Bartholomew, but then in the afternoon I played with blocks instead of watercolors and it would spark an interest in architecture and suddenly I wouldn't meet Bartholomew at painting camp like I was supposed to, and my soulmate was meant to be Gina from architecture college instead.

Except that theory breaks down in situations like—well, like this one, for example. If you're helping out with a bake sale and end up chopping up a lot of apples all at once in a line so Mrs. Wuthrich can sell a bunch of pies, like, does choosing a green apple over a red apple alter the course of fate? Because you'll get a different letter each time, and nothing happens in-between. I mean, I know I just got F twice, but this one probably—

Huh.

Anyway, sorry, I guess I shouldn't start going off about the existential crises of my childhood before we're even introduced. Nice to meet you! What's your name?

ANNA JONES

*The Chase*

There was something ahead of him, out on the open road. A moon, or a sun; a sphere of dull light, growing smaller as it moved. His eyes were prone to playing tricks on him, making shapes slip and slide and shake from his view, sometimes making them from nothing at all, but they were not playing tricks tonight. He was very old now, with hazy vision and a weary mind, but he knew for sure – and he didn't know much – that he wasn't alone, that the light he saw was true. He stepped off the curb and into the road, his pace quicker than it had been in some time, and set his tired eyes on the light.

It was a Sunday night in late December and the village was still. It sat in a post-Christmas slump, thick with icy silence, mourning the season it had waited a whole year for, so quickly gone. He could usually feel this sadness – the sadness of others soaked through him – but he couldn't now, with that light ahead. It seemed to shield him from the pain. He felt it enter him; first as a gentle throbbing right at his centre, and then as a smooth sensation rushing through him, all of him, from skin to bone.

The road was meant for cars, with a thick white line down its middle, though there were rarely any there, and there were none tonight, so he followed the line as if it had been painted for him. He had not taken this route to the village centre for many years, but he knew what he would find: the tired telephone box, slowly littering flakes of red paint onto the pavement, the pub on the corner with boarded windows, the dirtied bus stop. He would find broken things that had lived, briefly, and then died. That was how he saw it. And it was here, as these things did in fact appear before him, that the feeling focused in on his shoulders, his chest and eventually his heart.

Years ago, the man had been a father to a son. His son had white blonde hair, which met in a V-shape at the back of his head just above his neckline, like a tiny arrow. When guiding his son, reassuring him, soothing him, his hand had rested there. Rested with a light touch, the only touch that seemed right for his small son, whose eyes shined with the light of the huge world. It was for this reason that the V-shape remained in his mind, folded safely in its depths, coming to the surface now as that feeling began to press against his heart. He put a hand to his chest, to hold the feeling there, and the deeper it pressed, the more details of his son he remembered. They spilled out into the night, like secrets, and that's when he saw it. The tiny arrow. If he squinted, he could see it. If he squinted harder, he could see his son's thin shoulders too, and the milky bareness of his arms. All these parts of his son bled from his heart and found shape in the air, one by one, until all of his son was there, whole and complete.

A few weeks before, the man had reached a conclusion. He remembered it now, as he walked. It had come to him at the end of a string of thoughts that visited his mind regularly, ever since he was young, and tinted the lens through which he understood the events of his life. At the times of their arrival these thoughts seemed unrelated to each other; in their substance, that is, not in their nature. They were all ugly thoughts. Only now had their connection become apparent, and the final thought, where the string thinned and finished, was this:

Life was a chase.

Despite what this sentiment implied, and everything it complicated, he was relieved by its truth, which was, in itself, uncomplicated. He had been mowing the lawn when the conclusion struck him and he switched the machine off to honour the moment, resting a palm on the lawnmower's handle and tipping his chin towards the sunlight. Even finding those four words had been a chase for him. He was glad to have caught up with them, and hoped it marked the end of life's chasing.

Yet here he was again, chasing a light that, he realised, was now gone. Just like that. And chasing everything else, for he no longer knew where he was, so far from his home, and his wife, and that rare moment of clarity in the sunlight. Fear began to fill him, to take over him, slowing his step. He rolled his eyes over the dark, hoping they would hit a familiar bump in the blankness. After searching a while, hands flailing through the hollow air, it was clear that they would not.

When the man was a boy himself, his hands were good for nothing. That's what they told him, and that's what he told himself. He gripped loosely, pulled lightly, and let things slip. He had no grasp of life or how it should be lived. And as he grew into a man and raised a boy of his own, he touched the boy's head so softly it was almost no touch at all. He was scared to touch his son. He was scared of everything. It was probably this that killed the boy; the neglect, or the feeble attempt at love. And the tears of his wife that followed, he couldn't catch them.

He remembered how his large, clumsy hands tried and failed to fold comfort over her small shoulders, how they didn't fit right, how they only added to the weight.

It was those same hands now, fumbling around to find something that had been so close, so obvious, but finding nothing. Seconds, hours, maybe even days passed, just standing there, reaching. For what exactly, he didn't know. There was no feeling to be felt anymore, in or around him, only the post-Christmas slump that had been a part of him all along, hiding somewhere in the depth of him. It had waited to show itself, and here it was. The slump. He let his hands fall back to his side, and slowly opened his eyes.

He turned to face the way he'd come and, shyly, in sections, the country road revealed itself again: the zigzagged cracks in the concrete, the sodden, trampled leaves. He looked down at his empty hand to find that his fingers had become mysterious things; multiplying, and then vanishing; living and dying as he blinked. He stared at his hand until it was no longer a hand, but an entirely indecipherable thing that could be there, or not there. He didn't know, and he didn't care to. It no longer mattered.

MIRIAM HUXLEY

*Waning Gibbous Moon*

The dark canal is glittering, flickering lights from the houseboats lined up one after the other amongst the weeds. At night, this view transforms into something out of a fairy tale. Something picturesque, lacking the urban grime and rubbish that floats across the surface during daylight hours. The familiar sounds of the evening commute surround her: horns honk, bicycle bells ding, and she catches bits and pieces of conversation. She stops on the bridge, like she's waiting for someone or for something to happen. But nobody comes and nothing happens. And she stays, watching the moon – now just a sickle, a sharp crescent – rippling on the dark surface of the water.

Her flat is up a hill, not far from the canal, but enough of a walk to get her heart rate up. The dull thump echoes in her ears as she turns her key in the lock. The front door is black, the entryway dark, her building surrounded by a frame of scaffolding she can see just as much from the inside as the outside. A few days earlier, a letter crashed through her post box saying the building needed *essential repairs to the stonework*. Power cuts were to be expected. The foundation was mentioned. The word *crucial* underlined and in bold. She'd looked at the cost and felt a cold sweat. But, as her neighbours said, needs must. The work began soon after, starting with the assembly of the scaffolding.

In her flat, she goes about her normal routine, made more difficult in the dark, tidying her shoes away by feel, hanging her coat up on a hook she can't see but knows is there. She moves from room to room, leaving the curtains open, living by the light of the moon. Time measured by the waxing and waning of a natural satellite hundreds of thousands of miles away. That light illuminates the living room, turning the floorboards silver, a colour she never sees during the day. There's a part of her that wishes she could become nocturnal, like a bat or an owl, her eyes adjusting to the gradient shades of night. The light glints off the scaffolding, the metal exoskeleton keeping the building from collapsing in on itself. In this room, there's a crack on the wall that stretches from one end to the other. Someone attempted to camouflage the severity of the crack with patterned wallpaper, but look closely and you see ripples and tears. It's a peeling paper jungle she tries to ignore.

She stands by the window that once provided a view of the city and stares at the platform built just below the window ledge. Away at work all day, she doesn't see the workers climbing up the metal frame like bugs on a tree. She doesn't see them eating sausage rolls and crinkling bags of crisps, their legs dangling over the edge, unafraid of the long drop experienced by tumbling crumbs. She doesn't hear the buzz of saws or the staccato beat of many hammers.

Each night, she looks out at the scaffolding and searches for traces of them: tools forgotten, or jumpers hung over the metal, discarded when the sun made a short appearance and reflected off the windows.

She looks for progress. Her neighbours have been saying that the workers will disappear soon. Work like this doesn't carry on in the cold months. Too dangerous. They'll return once the worst of the winter weather subsides.

But the scaffolding will remain.

The neighbours joked about hanging Christmas decorations from the metal, wrapping lights around the front of the building, playing the scaffolding like tube bells. What else can they do but make the most of it?

She wonders if the moon has been shrinking before her eyes, the light changing. Soon, she'll look out at a half moon. She looks back at the scaffolding, so close she could open the window and climb out, let her feet dangle over the edge, watch her breath form tiny clouds in the moonlight. She puts a hand on the window frame, and just as she does, she thinks she sees something move from the shadows. She stares out the window, her face nearly pressed against the cold glass, trying to hold her breath so she doesn't fog up the pane. She thinks about calling her brother for a dose of his unshakeable sensibility. But he's away, practically unreachable. And besides, there's nothing there.

But one night, she comes home to a coffee cup from a fast-food chain perched on her windowsill. She imagines the cup getting knocked over, brown sludge pouring down the side of the building, creeping down her neighbours' windows. The next night, there's a sandwich wrapper, discarded crusts, a splat of tomato on the platform outside her bedroom window. A few nights later, a single glove.

Is it one person leaving these things? Is he always this forgetful? Maybe he has a car full of rubbish. A house left untidied. No system, no routine. And then she sees it again.

Movement.

But once more, there's nothing there.

On the night of the half moon, she meets one of her neighbours on the stairs. Jim. Or Tom, maybe. He introduced himself so long ago and although they talk most days, she can't remember that hurried first meeting. Now it would be too awkward to ask. But she knows he's the one who keeps up the shared garden. Sometimes, she spots him lugging bin bags up the stairs. Compost, she assumes, though they don't have a compost bin and he's going up, not out of the building. She tries not to get involved, tries to limit their interactions to passing in the hall and exchanging smiles.

Tonight, he doesn't smile.

'Did you hear?' he asks. His face is illuminated by the hall light they've all been complaining about. The light has gone wrong, yellow, and flickering, or sometimes it doesn't work at all. Now Jim (or Tom) looks yellow, his face all angles.

'Did I hear … ?' she repeats when she realises he's not going to say anything.

He runs a hand over his gaunt face – or maybe that's just the light. 'Never mind,' he says, the yellow light glinting on his teeth, 'I don't want to worry you.' Then he turns on his heel and returns to his flat. The hallway is momentarily bright, then the door closes, locks clicking into place, one after the other.

She climbs the stairs to her own door, unlocking three different locks with three different keys. The door swings open, a gaping mouth. She thinks of her neighbour's yellow face as she pushes the door shut. She locks each lock and pulls the chain across, not sure if she's keeping something out, or something in. She shakes her head. There's nothing but the sound of her own shoes on the floorboards. She goes about her routine, as usual, ending in the living room. The beam of moonlight is smaller, the face of the moon obscured by the ever-encroaching darkness. But the light still glints off the metal beams and posts, that carefully constructed structure she returns to each night. Tonight, she notices a paperback sitting close to the edge of the platform, the pages fluttering when the wind picks up. She imagines the forgetful builder, sitting there with his coffee and his tomato sandwich. And then she looks at the window, really looks, because there's palm prints, a faceprint. She can see them because the room is dark, and the moonlight is hitting the glass just right. They're on the outside, she's sure of it. She stares out the window, heart thudding, her face mirrored in the smudged glass. There's nothing there. There can't be, the workers left hours before she got home. But the book, the pages dog-eared.

She could go and stay at her brother's – she has a key. But he would tell her she's being silly, that she shouldn't run away from problems, that she should take action. She takes a deep breath and thinks about opening the window, creeping out onto the platform, proving to herself that there's nothing there. It's just a book, left behind by a forgetful builder, the kind of person who leaves his keys at home each morning. Tomorrow, when she's at work, he'll return and smile when he spots the book sitting where he left it. And soon, the builders will stop coming. The temperature drops each day. It's nothing. She should walk away, close the curtains, and switch the lights on. She isn't nocturnal; her eyes can't adjust. She's seeing things.

But just as she's walking away, there's a noise.

She's heard it before, this clanging, each night before she goes to bed. Her stomach drops. She reaches for her keys as she creeps back along the moonlit floor, towards whatever waits just beyond smeared glass.

TODD WORKMAN

*Divorce by Defenestration*


About the time he was falling

      head
      over
      heels,
            halfway between the first
                        and
                    second stories,
                    momentarily


        suspended


              in


                      diamond-like

        ringing
      fragments,


        he realized
            his sure-to-be-ex-wife
            was stronger than he was.

## TODD WORKMAN

*I always hoped that
one day he'd want me*


In my grandpa's backyard
was a stump
that looked like a lion,
with a mane of leafy offshoots,
lying sphinx-like in the grass.

I named him *Dad*,
fed him cookies
and secrets.

He in turn protected me
from loneliness
and secrets.

NICOLE CHRISTINE CARATAS

*Brontide*

The sea ebbs slowly, wrapping itself around her ankles. Toes dig into wet sand as she makes her way further into the water, her feet impervious to the rocks and broken shells that crunch beneath them.

Within the waves, she sees him. His face swirling beneath the midnight blue water, his pale brown eyes, the blond curls he always has to sweep back.

But then she blinks and he's gone, and there's nothing but the rolling seaweed, the white foam crashing onto the beach.

~

Kane and Morgana feasted on each other, clutching desperately for survival. She needed his touch, he needed hers. The first time they tangled, their bodies fused together, the welding so seamless it was hard to remember they had ever been two. Morgana's lungs collapsed, her stomach shrivelled, her arteries sputtered, and her brain went to sleep. The only part that remained was the pulsing of her heart, which echoed back from deep within Kane.

The heart that sustained him too.

~

Morgana's dress drags through the water, but she does not feel its growing weight. The sky above her threatens to crack open, but still she ventures out, out towards the call.

Her fingertips skim the water. The salt in the air clings to her hair, her eyelashes. It coats her nostrils as she inhales, dropping her head back until her hair follows her hands, dipping beneath the surface.

~

Kane slipped a delicate chain of twisted silver around Morgana's neck as he whispered, 'You'll never be free of me, Morgana.'

Her hand cradled the vial of his blood, entombed and still warm.

She did not wish for freedom.

Morgana sliced her own palm with a dagger, the blade carved from onyx. She licked her hand, letting her saliva dance with the blood, a slow and sensuous rumba on her tongue. Kane held an identical vial to her mouth, collecting the crimson potion and tying it around his own neck.

~

Morgana slips under, and her body dissolves. Submerged, she is weightless. No. Not weightless. *Boneless. Matterless.* Like each sinew that held her together has vanished, turned to salt water that washes away, drifting off to where it cannot be distinguished from the rest of the sea.

~

Kane loved nothing more than making his lists.

He listed all he loved about Morgana: her grey eyes,

her teeth grinding when she slept, the missing nail on her left pinky toe.

He listed all he wanted for them: a house that opened onto the beach, a promise that they would always be together, a joint funeral where they were buried at sea.

He listed his rules for Morgana: do not speak his name to others, do not wonder where he goes, do not ask him any questions.

Morgana adhered to them. She didn't think twice about it, not at first.

When he didn't come home at night, she kept her worries to herself. When he grew angry at her for doing the same, she convinced herself that he was overwhelmed and what he really needed was her.

So she spilled her blood for him.

And he thanked her.

~

When Morgana emerges, electricity crackles through her veins. She vibrates, a whirlpool spinning around her. Her hand clutches the onyx dagger, the black stone glinting against her ghostly pale skin. She drags it across her thighs, first the left, then the right. Blood trickles down her legs, mixing with the dark waters of the whirlpool. Water rises, a hurricane, and Morgana is the centre.

~

Kane tired of her.

He tired of her voice, her touch, her presence.

Morgana ripped the vials from their necks. She shattered them in her palm so his blood and her blood became *their* blood.

She clung to him, proffering the sweet crimson cocktail.

He peeled her off him like he was peeling off his skin. He stood before her, bloodied muscles and exposed bones. And like a banshee, she screamed, a primal, guttural sound so terrifying Kane reached for the salt.

~

The sky above rips open, the crash of thunder roars. But Morgana doesn't hear it. She hears only the call from within the water, the distant thrum she had long forgotten. She listens closely. It will tell her what to do, what she must offer in exchange for what she needs.

The hum grows louder, rivalling the forces in the sky that try to stop her. A bolt of lightning singes the beach, turning sand to glass, but does nothing to faze Morgana. She isn't afraid of the lightning. She is made from something stronger. She knows she can take on the lightning and win.

~

Kane cried silent tears as he left her there, crumpled on the porch of the house that didn't look out onto the water. He slammed into Zemyna, who had followed him without his knowledge. Zemyna was tall. That was all Morgana could see through her blood red vision. She watched that elongated figure take Kane into her arms, rub his back, spit in Morgana's direction. The wife Morgana could never be had come to collect him, come to save him.

The pair turned their backs on Morgana, fitting together like a femur into a pelvis.

~

Morgana feels them now, the cold, ancient spirits from deep within the waves. The lost sailors of old, and those older, so old their names are forgotten. Forgotten, but still there, still with her. She is a part of them. From their salty depths she emerged and to their salty depths she feels the call homeward.

She doesn't answer.

Instead, she makes her own call. She draws them up from the hidden places they've lingered for far too long.

The waves resist, refusing to give way to the spirits that rise. But the spirits come anyway. The swell cannot contain them.

They rise.

Morgana looks into faces she has never seen before yet knows better than her own. They stare back, unmoving but not static. They are ready to go where she bids them.

She steps forward, into them, a hazy veil, an icy chill consuming her, drawing her deep in the mass of spirits.

She is absorbed.

They know their purpose, know this reason for coming ashore. Overhead, thunder bellows a warning, rain wages war against the churning sea. The sky fights aimlessly, as if lightning could hold them back.

With Morgana at their centre, they move, a tidal wave upon the shore.

If it was a funeral at sea he wanted, then a funeral at sea he would get.

~

Kane wakes to a distant rumble, a growing thunderous caterwaul that he cannot quite place. Until it's too late.

They slash at his chest, the greedy feasting of long-buried creatures. They smack their lips as they devour his grey innards. In his final moments, he does not think to look for Zemyna nor Morgana. But it is Morgana he sees.

She's on the ceiling, watching, the corners of her mouth turned up, icy fire blazing in her eyes. Her legs are bloody, dripping down on him like a rusted faucet.

Morgana reaches towards the things consuming him, and suddenly, Kane feels airy and light, like gossamer caught in a breeze.

The creatures carry his body like guilt.

Teeth tear at his flesh, smaller spirits who haven't yet had a taste.

And then he is falling.

He thinks he might fall for eternity.

But then he sees a flash of midnight blue, a small ripple in an expanse of tranquillity.

As he breaks the surface, he hears her.

*You'll never be free of me.*

EMERSON ROSE CRAIG

*The Place of Lost Things*

I was dead for two months. Actually, I was dead for two months, seven days, and eleven hours. It happened over three decades ago, when I was nearly six years old. Mom and I were alone in the car when we crashed—or were crashed into, Mom can't remember. Her mind was too focused on me, tightly buckled in the back seat. Whiplash, sprinkled glass, and a minor concussion, but somehow no blood or breaks. We were lucky. That was all anyone could say. *You are so lucky*, plastered on the inside of grocery store get well cards that hung on the fridge until they were eventually forgotten under magnets, bills, and school drawings.

With the help of too much whiskey downed straight from the bottle, the story she had suppressed for decades comes pouring out. *I was too young to remember*, she begins, unable to look at me as memory takes over. All sixty-eight of those days had been carefully counted and then forced into the crevices of her mind in the unfulfilled hope of forgetting them. Her hands shake as she thinks back. It had been what I said; the words echoed inside her. *"Why would I be cold?"* as she led me out on a walk. *"The soul will be lonely,"* as she tried to put me to bed. *"What is this food supposed to taste like?"* while chewing listlessly on my favorite meal of pasta and parmesan. *"I don't understand why the body didn't die,"* on the way to a doctor's appointment. *"But your daughter is dead,"* as she pleaded with me to be myself again. And then, *"Mommy, I missed you,"* while she cried.

I tuck a blue and brown knit blanket around Mom's sleeping form on the couch, listening to her soft snores. I don't dare try and move her to her room. I don't want her to wake up. I gently rub my thumb on the deep crease between Mom's eyes until the tension eases in her face. Carefully, I tiptoe over to sit in a chair across from her. Her story was still so vivid for her, even after so many years. I tug at the bracelet on my wrist, spinning the lone plastic bead between my fingers as I watch her sleep. She never told me the story before, perhaps afraid of reawakening scars inside my mind. I wish she had not let them scar her so deeply instead.

Mom thinks I was too young, that I won't remember the two months I didn't smile or laugh, the days I spent wandering aimlessly and staring at nothing, the useless doctor visits. She says she was glad that I can't remember, thinks it is my mind's way of dealing with the trauma of the accident. It is better I don't remember. She looks so frightened thinking about it, her body limp on her worn-out couch, eyes wide and unfocused. I wonder if it would help if I told her the truth. She is right; I don't remember saying those things, or any of it. I do, however, remember the sound of the shattering glass, burning rubber, and Mom screaming my name. And I remember the darkness.

It wasn't the dark of night. Although I was afraid of the dark, it was familiar; something that I knew. This was different. This darkness was thick. It made my movements slow. I could see nothing around me, but my hand remained visible as I stretched my fingers out into it. I couldn't see—Where was Mommy? I screamed for her, but she did not come. I sobbed, alone in the darkness with my arms wrapped tightly around my knees.

Eventually, I grew tired of waiting. I crept along with tear-stained cheeks. I moved slowly but steadily, my short legs never growing tired in the endless onward. Change came in the form of a damp squish beneath my sandals. It was a single sock. But it wasn't mine. All my socks had pink or purple tipped toes. This sock was blue and white. After that, more objects appeared: bits of ribbon, a plastic wheel, a pair of glasses, an umbrella, an earring, a retainer, a battery, a mug. They were littered on the floor of darkness; a room no one had cleaned in too long.

I continued on, and so did the items, but I couldn't find Mommy. I kicked at objects as I passed them, surprised that nothing made a sound, not even a string of keys that I managed to kick in front of me for several paces before they were lost to the wayside of things. None of the things were mine, they belonged to others, but those others were not here. I was here, with the things in a darkness we shared. I was alone but for pennies and chargers.

I kicked a small rain boot with a ladybug face painted on the toe from my path. As it landed on its side, it spat something from its depth at my feet. A little white bead that had been carefully tied to the center of a thick piece of silky neon pink string. I dangled it before my face and watched it turn slowly, revealing a black P inked on one side of the plastic bead. P for Penelope, Mommy had said.

Mommy wasn't there to tie it neatly in place. I had once tried to show Mommy that I could tie it all by myself, but it had slipped away at the park. Mommy hadn't been able to find it, even though she'd looked hard. She'd said it was gone. I didn't want it to slip away again, so I tucked it into my pocket. It would be safe there, and Mommy would be glad it was found. I looked harder at the items as I passed them, but none of them were mine so I didn't take them; a teddy bear, a baseball glove, a pencil, a jacket, a watch, a hat. I wanted to find more that was mine or Mommy's. I didn't want them to be alone in this place of lost things anymore.

For the first time, my limbs began to feel tired. The darkness grew thicker around me, pushing against me as I walked. My movements slowed further, as though I were walking through Jell-O. I kept searching. I didn't want any of my things to be alone anymore. My feet began to hum as the darkness beneath me vibrated. A loud crack sounded around me. I covered my ears in pain. It had been so long since I had heard sound. The darkness beneath me gave out, sending me tumbling alongside a flip-flop, a screw, and a diamond ring. I reached out, trying to grab hold of anything, but it was only darkness. I wasn't done searching. What if there was more that needed to be found?

I remember blinking as the light hurt my eyes. I remember the carpet felt itchy under my legs. I remember the curly-haired doll Mom was holding before me, a pleading look in her eyes. I remember I hugged her, and she cried. I remember saying, *"Mommy, I missed you."*

HAYLEY BERNIER

*It's Thursday and I haven't written*


because I barely know how to sleep
with all these teeth in my mouth.
I count them like the days,
December leaning over
my shoulder to breathe
along the gap of my collar
and whisper nightmares into my skin,
lost Christmas gifts, a maze-house on fire,
aliens sitting at the table.

I've been clenching my jaw so tight
my doctor tells me
maybe there are a few words
I don't want to say,
so I keep space
folded
in my mouth
until my head billows through
the morning
ringing with gaudy winter.

If the sky was as bright as the snow
I would not feel an ache,
a restlessness that runs
as fast as the muse flickering in my peripheral.
If only it would hold still.
A flame guttering with prayer,
a hope for something good: convulsing.

HAYLEY BERNIER

*There is a hallway in my mind*


There is a hallway in my mind
and down it, I always look.

I'm walking between closing walls
and both my elbows begin to crook.

I see its ugly rough carpet,
hear the shudder of the slamming door

at the end where he was inside with her.
The silence has a face, implores—

another intrusion of my mind
walks me back down this strange and harrowed

unsettling stillness: crackling static,
needles in my skin, bones, marrow.

My mind traverses this place
like so much water seeps into pipes.

But waterlines score the stoney banks
with countless layered stripes,

and this house is on the shore
built from two, with a fissuring seam,

anomalous windows and flickering faerie lights,
pulsing out of tune, some uncanny dream—

Fingers pushing into plaster proving
that every trap I found myself inside

had been formed by my hands alone.
Not man. Not moon. Not ravenous, swirling tide.

## HAYLEY BERNIER

*Nothing to Fear*

but I was
about to get into the shower
when I see a daddy longlegs
sitting near the drain
and with a pang
I think of the distress in your eyes:
gritty from the camera
and frantic-wide as you describe
the grip of arachnophobia
on your breathing.
Spiders are what I am
protecting you from;
would have been one of my roles
in your life, a reason to keep me
yours. But we never got there.
I gently push the falling water
over the spider, a tiny tidal tithe
and as it slides out of view,
I hear you tell me
that to drown them is not enough,
that it will merely seal into a ball,

protect its body during the calamity
of warm water and pressure
and when the tsunami ends,
the spider will uncurl
and climb all the way back
to the bathtub it came from.
Even so, I flood it.
I send it draining away
hoping that maybe
you were simply wrong.

JULIA GUILLERMINA

*The Front Row*

I almost arrived late to the funeral, but they waited for the last of us.

Everyone was already seated, wearing silent faces. I had walked here with a group from the bus station. We were those who didn't own mourning clothes. I had found this burgundy jumper, sober enough.

There weren't many seats left. The others went to stand at the back of the room. It concealed their rainbowy allure from sight. I spotted a free seat in the first row and, after a moment of hesitation, I weaved in and out between the benches and sat there.

I didn't dare look back at the group I had come with.

The master of ceremony stopped the soft music that filled the lack of conversations. The hush felt deafening.

'Welcome,' her microphone voice punched my eardrum, 'you who have come to honour Marina's memory.'

There were Marina's siblings, her mother, her favourite teacher. Everyone felt the absence of Marina's father, who died five years before. Some friends of the family had managed to come, from all across the country.

I imagined they were all thinking of their memories of Marina. They would have so many: Marina at six mispronouncing words, like all children do. Marina at ten running barefoot on the pebbles. Marina at twelve, starting the trumpet and annoying every neighbour. Marina at fifteen, bringing back a cat from the street and convincing everyone to take care of him – Louis. We had organised a party for his first birthday.

The master of ceremony called Liz, Marina's mum, to the pulpit. She walked tall, and when she spoke, her voice didn't shake. Her eyes were clear. She knew what to say. Maybe she had started her husband's funeral with the same words. When she unfolded her paper, I breathed.

'I feel so lucky to have known Marina,' she said with a smile.

I didn't. If I hadn't met her, I wouldn't be here. What a horrible thing, funerals. I was glad I wouldn't go to my own.

The people I could see had soft expressions. Their eyes had that glisten, their nose had that redness. Moistened skin around the nostrils and the mouth, wet and disorganised lashes.

I wasn't crying. My life wasn't changing that much. I didn't know Marina eight months ago.

Liz went back to her seat and Marina's brother took the lead. He, who looked so much like his sister, he insulted her. Out loud. I hadn't had the chance to meet him before the funeral, but I had heard about him. He was known as a shy guy, more interested in computers than people. But grief has a strong hold. One of the things it does is make you angry. Marina's brother started crying mid-sentence, as if he was shocked by what he'd just said. I couldn't look at him and see his despair.

A man whispered behind me, 'How unfair. How young a girl.'

She was young indeed. We all were. My mum had said it over the phone. And Liz. And this man. *This isn't normal. You shouldn't have to live this at your age.*

Well, then, make it stop.


A song started playing. Liz and Marina's friends had asked me to help choose one, but what did I know about songs for Marina? The only thing I had ever listened to with her were funny songs not appropriate for a funeral. The others knew better. They had found the one.

'You were born in my head,' the song said, 'You now live in my skin.' A chill ran between my goosebumps. It was racing across them, barefooted. It came smiling. It started in my head and ended up in my belly. It had painted all my back blue.

I felt the urge to turn around, to go out and check. Marina must be there somewhere. I could sense her. She was going to be there and say we looked stupid dressed like we did. She would come near me, with her crooked smile and her big nose and she would comment on my clothes.

'Is that the best outfit you could find in your closet?'

I had to leave. This ceremony was not for me. I could see everyone there wouldn't mind me going, just as they didn't mind me staying. Why was I there, anyway?

'June will read something now,' the master of ceremonies said, and I couldn't fly away anymore. Liz looked at me, with her nice cheeks, rounded by her kindness. Liz, who I had met that day I was so afraid. Liz who had realised I needed a napkin when I didn't dare ask for it. Liz who had known I would only want water because she was *the parent*. Liz who had rung me first, to tell me the news.

'June,' she had pronounced, calm, and I had already known there was a problem, because why else would Liz call me?

I stood up.

She had said to all of Marina's friends that we could write something if we wished, as if she'd known that I wanted to. Not for Marina, but for the others. For the living. For Liz.

The more steps I took towards the pulpit, the farther it felt.

I had written anecdotes. This day, and that day, and Marina's humour, her crooked smile, her mischief. I couldn't think of anything else and people were going to wonder. Who is that girl in that red jumper and why was she asked to read?

I couldn't write about myself. I would never say out loud I felt good because she liked me. I felt powerful because she wanted to spend time with me.

I couldn't write about her lips on my lips. I hadn't been so sure of loving her back. Loving her for who she was, like love is supposed to be. She was just a girl, a beautiful girl infatuated with me.

I couldn't write about the warmth of her body. How could I admit it haunted me? I still felt it when I closed my eyes, like it had stuck with me.

MALINA SHAMSUDIN

*The Cleaner*

## EVER AFTER SERVICES
☆☆☆☆☆ **430 HelpMe reviews**
**Trauma Cleaning & Biohazard Removal in**
**the Dark Forest • Open 24 hours •**
**Phone: 1800-KEEP-IT-CLEAN**

'Very professional and able to accommodate the urgency of the situation. Ella and her team went above and beyond during my time of grief. Without them, I don't know how I would have made it through this.'
– *Ms Snow W., Dark Forest* (Verified Customer)

**About the business:**
At EVER AFTER, we address situations that may upset the conventional cleaner. Our highly trained technicians regularly carry out trauma, death, and crime scene cleaning tasks for emergency services, social services, landlords, as well as commercial and industrial companies. Be it incidents of self-harm, hoarding, or homicides, our discrete task force works through a rigorous five-step process to restore a safe home environment or workplace.

•

## STEP 1: ASSESSMENT

It's quite common to gravitate towards a profession due to parental influence. Perhaps less common is choosing a career because you had to scrape your deceased father off the floor of a garden shed. There's more to that story of course, but as anecdotes go, not many acquaintances – or potential significant others – have the stomach for it. And as it happens, even if they say they do, they really don't.

*'Good women don't … mess with bodily fluids.'*

Fortunately, my clients appreciate the work that I do. This is partly thanks to my long-serving crew members Jack and Gus. Vegan Jack tells tall tales – like attributing his bald pate to a youthful indiscretion with a woman larger than life. He brings experience in 'giant' catastrophe clean-ups and excels in hard-to-reach places. Despite his restricted palate, he has a strong aversion to green beans and herbaceous stalks because 'they just invite trouble'. Petite Gus handles pest control. Once a rising amphibian biologist, his career came to a fork when vandals broke into his lab to fling endangered frogs against the walls. As backstories go, we're an odd bunch that complement each other. After more than 400 cleaning jobs together, we've developed an advanced shorthand. What gets us through the day-to-day gruesomeness is knowing that our toil is a small contribution towards lending the dead or injured a shred of dignity while allowing those left behind to recoup and possibly imagine some sense of normalcy.

Today, my crew and I are tackling the home of one Mr. Beest. According to his housekeeper (my client), the homeowner had been 'up to the usual tinkering while

Mrs. Beest was away' and accidentally shot himself in the collar bone while cleaning an antique pistol. The paramedic report implies a discrepancy, but I respectfully defer to my client's version of events. Mr. Beest is fighting for his life in the hospital, and anything that helps my client get through that trauma alone is all that matters.

As we enter the grand empty house, I am immediately overwhelmed by the scent of rose in the foyer. I abhor roses and resent the various cluttered floral arrangements' poor efforts to mask the pervading scent of iron from the next room ... and oddly, the scent of wet dog. I am certain the client said nothing of domestic animals and note none of the usual pet paraphernalia in the vicinity. The fourth finger on my left hand starts to cramp.

'To the right, to the right!'

I barely manage to jump out of the way as Gus barrels into the space with our gear, followed by Jack's steadier stride. The regime begins.

## STEP 2: BIO REMOVAL

We are now wearing azure hazmat suits, shoe covers, and latex gloves. Each suit only offers protection for one hour, so we set the timer. Our ventilator hums, protecting against airborne pathogens and smells. You never get immune to the job requirements; you just get better at bracing yourself before stepping in.

The worksite is a library with vaulted cherry ceilings, mahogany millwork, and an imposing fireplace. Above the fireplace is a set of antique firearms, with the conspicuous outline of a missing item. Books fill every shelf. No photographs. An out-of-place chandelier crowds the ceiling. The prisms of colourful light coming from an ornate window instil a sense of claustrophobia. I walk closer and see that it is an amalgamation of small hand-blown glass flora in mutated shapes and sizes. This would be hell to clean. I hope Jack does not notice the beanstalk motif.

'Much better,' says Gus, filling the room with our more conducive industrial light. We see the extent of the biological products then. It is concentrated at the end of the room directly opposite the glass window, near the wrought iron fireplace. It is on the floor, in the grate, on the mantel, on the wallpaper, on the footstool and the leatherback chair. A solitary side table holds a single forgotten meal: cold steak, congealed potatoes ... and green beans. I swoop in to cover the plate, pretending to right an empty decanter on the floor. Despite my efforts, Jack gags as he crosses the room.

We are looking for shards of bone, blood, body fluid, hair, and a bullet. It can be difficult to do this job effectively if you do not have the correct information and tools – including a good playlist. Gus selects Queen's *Bohemian Rhapsody* to kick us off.

As the crew address the mantel and walls, I sift through the ashes in the fireplace to find a shard of collar bone. More sifting, and I unearth a small circular object. It's a gold ring. There's a strange temptation to try it on. Would it fit like mine used to? I toss it quickly into a ziplock bag, flexing my left hand like it burns.

There's shattered glass. Carefully, I extract the ombre shards and place them in a newspaper. A snow globe, perhaps?

No – an anatomically correct lamp sculpture of a hollow heart, I deduce, pulling at the charred remains of wire. Any interior designer worth their salt would balk at its gaudiness, but I cannot help but imagine how the piece must have been when it was whole, with clever lights illuminating the organ from within – as if pulsing with a life force. Perhaps this heart was faulty and didn't have the passion to shine. I imagine pressure around this heart, until with a sigh of defeat, the fragile ornament shatters.

*'I'm sorry you think I'm hurting you. I'm only trying to protect you.'*

I shake my head. I'm getting fanciful. The broken heart is wrapped in paper. My chest hurts, and I feel a light sweat under the hazmat suit.

The alarm shrills the hour. Gus gives me a careful hand up, and the three of us regroup outside in the hall, sharing a flask of tea and a roll of antacids as we coordinate the next steps. Jack announces that he will be adding a beneficiary to his insurance plan: his Harper is having a 'gosling'. As delighted as I am for Jack, I feel … is it envy that someone got it right? My left hand feels like it's on fire. I massage the naked fourth finger.

Gus pipes up with his own delightful news: pakora power at the local. It is a 2-for-1, including a chef special of six veg and meat mixes.

We toast to goslings and pakoras, then change our suits to Blue Swede's *Hooked on a Feeling*. A painkiller chases my antacid just in case. I would kill for chocolate.

## STEP 3: THREE-STEP CLEANSE

Jack finds the missing bullet lodged into a first edition of Lord Byron's *The Bride of Abydos*. Why the obsession with doomed historical romance?

'Fickle and overrated – that's what love is.' I flush

in embarrassment at having spoken aloud and focus on scooping up the inordinate amount of hair under the skirting. I think they will ignore me.

'When it's right, it *is* all that it's cracked up to be,' Jack responds softly, almost defensively. 'The problem is when we confuse "extreme like" or "maybe love" for the real thing. Forcing either only does harm.'

Gus adds, 'Amphibians aren't the most faithful lovers. But there's one species of poisonous Peruvian frog – *Ranitomeya imitator* – that chooses to be monogamous. Some theorise that when these frogs find their mate, the toxins in their body commingle to produce a chemical akin to euphoria. That's got to be love, right?'

Jack coughs with a slight shake of his head, forcing Gus to raise his voice: 'I'm an optimist. I just keep swiping right, hoping someday they'll notice I'm worth at least a kiss.'

The steam in my goggles is too much. I excuse myself to the kitchen and am surprised to find my lashes wet and cheeks moist.

## STEP 4: EXTRACTION

Once, I had maybe-love. There was a meet-cute and random things in common. He even claimed to like my work anecdotes. My mistake was allowing him to tag along on an emergency call. Then again, I knew he wouldn't wait in the car.

He had been quiet. One glance, and I knew he did not have the mental resources to cope. Later, he pulled away in the silence of the car:

> *'I thought you helped people, Ella. I thought you were a bloody glorified maid. This is worse …'*

I remember the scent of crushed roses underfoot as my heart shattered. I reach out, willing him with every fibre to see that I remain the same person, that I never lied or misrepresented myself.

> *'Look ... I love you. If we were to make this work,*
> *maybe ... maybe you could start something new.*
> *Or not work at all ... I'll take care of you.'*

~ Maybe-love is not love. It's like ... mock meat. It only works if you are willing to suspend disbelief. Even then, you convince yourself that it is not all bad ... as an alternative for the real thing. You make do for a greater good. Surely there is no greater good than me? I deserve more than an alternative.

'You're *ending this?*'

Charming, isn't it? The incredulity in his voice tamed the sting. The fault was clearly mutual. I loved that he loved me. I did not think to check if I loved him back. I am guilty of letting him believe what he wanted to.

He kept the ring; I kept the shoes. We remain friends – I mute his socials, as he does mine. Last I heard, he was dating a podiatrist.

'To the right, to the right.'

It's Gus. I have left the hot water running on my left hand. He slides me to the right, away from the sink. He turns off the faucet, gently wrapping a towel around my pinkened left hand. I mumble something about early onset arthritis, convincing no one. He turns to quietly wipe the counter, nudging another towel towards me. Discreetly tucked into the biohazard face towel is a bag of multi-coloured chocolate buttons. I'm about to say something when we're interrupted.

'Can someone cover those damned beanstalks?'

## STEP 5: WRAP-UP

I'm crunching on the chocolate buttons in my car. The job's done, my crew has headed home. I send a quick update to my client, asking after Mr. Beest. As I snap in my seat belt, my phone chimes with a response:

> Great news about finding the ring!
> Mr B is out of surgery and perked up now
> Mrs B is here. Thank goodness this old dog
> has some bite left.
> Bless you, Ella!

I put my car into reverse with a smile and pull out of the driveway.

> *'I'm an optimist. I just keep swiping right, hoping someday they'll notice I'm worth more than a kiss.'*

> 'To the right, to the right.'

Huh. I quit crunching the buttons, trying to savour the moment. The rich chocolate melts slowly in my mouth. Cocoa butter, the real thing.

As I change gears into drive, I think ... I have a lot to think about.

My radio kicks in: Electric Light Orchestra's *Mr Blue Sky*. It's a beautiful new day, hey, hey.

DAVID BLAKESLEE

## The Lot Lizard and the Wrecking Ball

*Lot Lizard: A sex worker that operates out of the parking lot of a truck stop*

*Wrecking Ball: A heavy object; something that sweeps away everything in its path*

2 AM and the road had taken him to the old familiar place along the highway. He hauled his body out of the cab and into the cheap room where the lot lizard joined him, like she had so many times before. He knew her well after the last few years. She was the only constant at any of the stops. He knew what to expect from her. The birthmark underneath her left eye, the tiny chip in her front tooth.

She knew his hands, how they shook before he touched her. This place was always good for business because the owners either didn't care or were getting a piece of the profits from Julio. She turned on the usual charm. Only the nice ones would spring for the rooms. A bed you can rent by the hour, with the smell of decades of cigarette smoke seeping out of the wallpaper. Most take it in the cab of their truck where they eat and sleep and fart and piss in bottles if there's nowhere to stop. He said he needed to get some actual shuteye and it's never the same in the rig. He removed his shirt. She ran her hand along his belly, stroked his balding head, gave him what he paid for.

After, they lay together, their minds wandering the avenues of neurons so recently set on fire by the brief application of familiar routines. Images and patterns passed through their heads, still-life portraits of their pasts and hardships.

*Broken noses, bleeding*
*gums*

        *Mangled minivans,*
        *decomposing animals*

*Yellow bruises and*
*shared needles*

        *A pill to wake you up, a*
        *pill to get you hard, a pill*
        *to put you back to sleep*

*A screaming man*
*who doesn't know his*
*limits; clenched fists*

        *A bicycle without a rider,*
        *wheels upturned on the*
        *side of the road*

*One backpack*
*containing everything*
*you own*

        *Boot on the gas pedal*

*Dirty fingernails*
*counting bills*

*No text messages, no*
*missed calls*

Then, in a moment of sweetness, he asked the question. The naive question that some of the men ask in the stupor of post-coital bliss. They don't really mean it when they ask, because if the answer was yes, they wouldn't know the first thing to do to actually make it happen. Still, it was nice of him to consider her. Of course she thought about it once or twice before, but fantasies are dangerous. Ten miles down the road he might change his mind and get rid of her. He could be someone else in some other city. Men can change like that in an instant. Julio was nice at first. Look how that ended up.

He probably shouldn't have asked, he didn't mean to vocalize it, it just slipped out. Hell, why not? He didn't have much else going on. He took the job because Amanda had wanted to make a down payment on the Victorian fixer-upper. It was 3 months before she realized that it wasn't just a new house she had wanted. He'd stayed on because it was the only thing he was good at. She would probably find him boring and jump ship at the first stop. He never knew how to talk to women, or anybody. He didn't keep in touch with people. He did most of his routes in complete silence. No radio, no interview shows. If he found a stretch of highway long enough, not even his own thoughts came through.

Maybe he was different. He seemed more timid than most. Some of them came to her because they were angry. They sought revenge against a specific woman, but for the physical element, any woman would do. Some came to her because they found themselves too stupid or ugly to think they could get it anywhere else. Some were just plain horny. He came because he was lost. The first time he saw her, he didn't even know what he wanted. He didn't know who to pay or when. He spoke to her softly. But he was still one of them, no matter how he might seem. He would barrel through her life and disappear in the other direction.

They were both certain that it would all be a wreck in the end. Despite their hesitation, for a few precious moments the images changed.

*A chain link fence*

        *A two-car garage*

*A seat by a window,*
*with a bookcase nearby*

        *Friends over on weekends,*
        *holidays and game days*

*A dog they could spoil*

        *A bed with two impressions;*
        *a bathtub with two different*
        *kinds of shampoo*

Julio would have to be dealt with. But girls had disappeared before, and so long as they didn't owe him too much money, he never went to much effort to track them down. They were all replaceable. No shortage of young flesh; no shortage of desperate situations. When girls dropped off the map, she always assumed the worst.

And sometimes it was true. Everyone saw the stories. But other times they were never found. Had they gotten out? Maybe they had just been in the right place at the right time.

She probably didn't want his help. Most girls didn't. Some girls if you asked them something like that, they'd laugh at you, or start to get suspicious. More than once, he had been accused of being a cop. He was too quiet. They mistook that for judgment. Really, he didn't think of them as any different from the guy inside flipping the greasy burgers, or the lady at the counter hawking pills under the table. You don't ask them too many questions, or tell them they should quit. He sacrificed himself for the company every week. Because people like stuff, and they like their stuff to arrive quickly. We all expect a certain amount of sacrifice to be made for our own convenience. Everyone uses the skills they were given. But he asked her anyway. Maybe it was the familiarity that made him so bold.

The silence continued. She didn't answer because she didn't want to let him down. She played with the curly black hair on his chest. He let his hand rest on her ass, an act of intimacy that she wouldn't let anyone else get away with. The digital clock glowed red next to them, a lighthouse beckoning them back to shore. She would need two more before morning to make her nightly slice. She went to the toilet and then slipped on her clothes and shoes. He gave her the money, and when she went back to the lot, she noticed that he had hidden something between the bills.

It was the spare key to the truck. She could hide until they had cleared the state line, if she wanted to. She knew his rig. Either way, tomorrow was waiting. He had the room for a few more hours so he tried to fall asleep. Just on the precipice, he saw a road stretched out before him, a wide open sky above. Around any corner there might be obstacles; behind every fence there might be something ready to leap. He saw his dashboard, his controls. He tested the clutch and the brake. He drifted off to the open highway, knowing that the heavy load doesn't need to bring destruction so long as it is handled with care.

KATIE HAY-MOLOPO

*Potsherds: A Poem, in Two Parts*

## I.

Are you sure you mean it?

> When you say those words
> "Thy will be done"
> > over and over to your journal.

> > You'll run out of ink soon.

Do you hear yourself?

> The same phrase thrown against the wall.

> > > I'm surprised there isn't a hole there
> > > that you haven't worn out your knees
> > the backs of your hands
> where your fingers interlaced rub        your skin.

Why are you nervous?

> I thought you said you believe this stuff.
> "The door will open at its appointed time."
> > > *Appointed time.*
> > > Who talks like that?

I thought you said you were ready
                    to accept His will
                            (whatever that is).
"Whatever pleases the potter!"
                    you said.

                        Yet look at you

                back where you started
            sitting with your face in the sun
        eyes squeezed shut

                so if he asks you to look at him
            you can blame the tears
                on the light.

## II.

i am sitting alone when my Father appears he says son
come with me there's something important i need to
show you so i pick myself up and follow him through the
door past the clamor the roar of the market down a ways
to the potter's house and there he stops and prompts tell
me what you see and i look and i say i see a man with
hands like the heavens raising valleys to mountainous
heights extricating light from abyssal oblivion i see a
man squeezing the soil so tenderly violently that the
clay in his hands it's beginning to breathe i watch the
mud slather itself over immaculate skin catching under
the man's fingernails grinding itself into the crevices
of his palms the wrinkles between his knuckles until
it seems that the man and clay are one caught up in a
strange dance of stretching and bending a deconstructive
transformation and as i watch spellbound my Father
he turns to me and he asks what do you think my son
this clay would say if it could speak i consider the man
attending to his wheel responding to the clay as if it can
feel every dip and every rise every slice from the potter's
knife every intrusion of his fingers i consider them and
i wonder in the crafting and the shaping is there ever
a point where maybe just maybe the clay says o potter

how i love the wonder of your touch but if i'm made for this then please tell me why it hurts so much i wonder if there are moments when it just wants to run tell the potter it's done being shattered and fashioned just to be smashed again i wonder if the clay fancies itself an ornate vase the kind that one would place on a pedestal in a home decorate with precious stones and if it knew its destiny was just to be a crude lamp designed to brighten the potter's night and be filled with oil only to be burned given charred black edges i wonder would it turn to the potter and make a different proposition i know were i in its position i certainly would try but as i watch i realize this bodily vessel of mine is not so noble as this ugly unformed pliable piece of dirt this handful of earth with nothing to prove proving its worth by humbling itself to this man with hands like the heavens perfection unafraid to mingle with dust this lump of clay surrendered complete submission totally trusting in the process my Father asks again what says the clay my son i say *a e dirwe thato ya gago*

thy will be done

LAUREN N. THURMAN

*Initiation*

On a late October afternoon, a girl took the long way home from school. She walked along a path that wound through the hills near her subdivision, the trail dipping in and out just enough that a person using it might occasionally fall out of sight of the road. It was a path well suited for wallowing. And for disappearing.

Penny trudged along, looking at her feet, reliving the humiliating scene that had taken place in eighth period. McKenna Crawford hadn't meant to be hurtful—not that Penny could know this—but the way she'd said *virgin* with that pitying little pout had sunk Penny into a deep self-conscious agony until the bell signaled their release.

Penny watched the rocks on the trail as she muttered half-formed insults to the memory of McKenna's stupid smirk. (McKenna, of course, had already forgotten about the whole exchange.)

Some distance down the trail, a crow squawked three times. Penny looked up on the third, and something about the way its profile straddled the horizon made her stop. The scene she had been running through her head, with all its embellishments and reinventions, vaporized into so much crisp fall air, leaving only the crow. Black cutout in a wide blue sky.

After a few moments she started moving again, this time with her eyes up. She took in the afternoon sunshine and the sounds of the tall grasses whispering on the hillside. Her mother, if she saw this, would have been pleased—not only because it meant Penny was more aware of her surroundings, but also because she was less absorbed in her thoughts. She was the sort of teenager whose mind seemed desperate to be anywhere except above her feet.

But in this moment, Penny was doing her best to notice the things around her, to keep her thoughts from flitting off somewhere else. She noticed, for example, that the crow was still there. It had flown a few feet down the trail and stopped. It squawked again, three times, like a phone alarm. Penny wrinkled her brow and kept walking.

The third time this happened—the crow alighting in her path and calling out three times—the wind shifted. And Penny recognized, finally, that this was an invitation. The crow was calling her to follow it. If she chose. But what was the other choice? Walk straight home to her chores and her homework, go back to school the next day to face McKenna's smirk again? The thought of the posters on her bedroom wall, the flowery bedspread she'd had since middle school, made her cringe. They were predictable. *She* was predictable. Halfway through high school and she'd never done anything beyond what was expected of her. But if she followed that crow...

Of course, there was only one choice she was ever going to make.

Penny smiled and lurched forward, stumbling a little on loose rocks, and chased after the bird as it jumped into the air and veered right, landing on a hill far away from the trail. She ran it down, but it took off for a jutting crag of rock just beyond and she smiled, because wasn't this just like an adventure. Wasn't she going to leave behind the chafing quietness of a life wedged between school and home—a little girl's life—and plunge into a new world where things were great and dire. She just had to let the crow take her to the beginning of her journey. She just had to begin.

And if it ended up leading nowhere, well then she could always go back to the trail, back to her house, back to her normal Tuesday afternoon, before her parents even got home.

She came to the top of the last hill she had seen the crow dive behind, but it was gone. Before her lay a mighty crack in the ground whose jagged rocks staggered down into an unknowable darkness, to unseeable depths. This was it; she knew it was. This was where it started.

She picked her way down to the hole and knelt carefully to peer over the edge. Her eyes strained to see farther into the abyss, but it was only black that swam before her. A gentle, warm wind came from below, making her hair dance around her cheeks. She did not notice that her foot was slowly extending over the chasm and stretching down, down, toward the first shelf of rock below the grass.

Cold fingers dug into her shoulder. She was wrenched back onto the hillside where her head smacked hard against the ground. A man stood over her, black cutout in a wide blue sky.

She sat up and scrambled back, a little dazed, to try to look at him properly. Hades was tall, young, vibrant but somehow colorless. He sucked on a cigarette and regarded her without urgency. When Penny's hand came up reflexively to cover her nose, he dropped the cigarette to the ground and stamped it out with a gray sneaker.

"What do you think you're doing?" he asked.

"I was following a crow and it brought me here," she explained. "So I'm going to go down into the pit. I think I'm supposed to."

"Were you now. Are you now." He began to walk in a slow circle around her.

It occurred to her, then, that she was far from the trail, alone in the hills, with Hades. A shiver wriggled up the backs of her arms. It echoed through the grasses on the hills and up into the darkness of the trees beyond, a soft, expectant ripple of things that have been holding their breath, waiting for the season to turn.

"Anyway it's not a pit," Hades said from somewhere behind her. "It's a door. It's *my* door. Do you know what's on the other side?" He returned to her front and looked down at her, his legs blocking her view of the crack in the earth.

She thought it might be a good idea to turn around and go home now. But if she did that, she wouldn't be able to answer his question. And everything would be exactly the same as it always was.

"I mean, I guess I'll find out. That's like the whole point."

Penny got to her feet and dusted off her hands. She took a step toward him, lifting her leg high and stomping down to shake courage up her shins and into her stomach.

Hades took a deep breath to find patience and then he closed the remaining distance between them, fast and cunning as a paper cut. His eyes bore down; his breath plumed over her nose and mouth.

Sliding a gray tongue over gray lips, he said, "This door only opens one way. Are you prepared to walk through? Are you ready to cross into the shadow and never look at the same sky again, Penny?"

Her name was a toy in his mouth. She found it painful to meet his eyes, so she looked at the torn seam in the ground behind him, where darkness pulsed like the heartbeat of a living thing. His breath continued to fall on her face and she felt her cheeks glow red under his shadow. Her lips prickled from the closeness of his mouth. In her gut roiled a slick mass that lurched from terror to hunger to a cold sort of knowing. She was teetering between worlds: Behind, the trail and her house and its door that locked. Ahead—below—the mouth of the unknown. And the only thing standing in her way was a pair of gray eyes, which seemed to either warn or mock depending on which one she looked into. Left or right, push forward or turn back. She had to choose. Now, and here.

But there was only one choice she was ever going to make.

Hades saw all this taking place within her and moved aside. Penny set her jaw and took three steps to the edge of oblivion. He followed close behind, his colorless body like static electricity all along her back and legs. She would not tremble. She would not let him see her tremble.

Beneath her, infinity unfolded its hands and invited her down. She lowered one leg to the rock she had almost reached last time and, pausing, turned back to look up at Hades, who was shaking his head and huffing a low chuckle, as though he couldn't believe this shit.

The underworld's warm breath lapped at her shins and she took another slow step.

ANTHI CHEIMARIOU

*Portraits of a Couple*


Rainbow lights like the ones you see on the
road at night when you squint your eyes.
She chose to ride on the back of this bike.

A lovely cloud, the one that when it dissipates,
reveals her eyes more clearly: a cloud of toxins
she releases into the world; I want to see her      lungs.

A fight, a bottle flying across the room,
the happiest marriage. The dog's food left outside.
She is seen eating every slice of the red-velvet cake

left from the reception, as if her life depended
on the action of picking up the fork and pushing
it down her throat. I imagine it was a good one.

He asks her to take a polaroid of him next
to the waves – ribs suspended in mid-air.

# ANTHI CHEIMARIOU

## Red Onion

Your layers,

thick and thin,
uncovered purple flesh.
that makes your masters cry;

a cry so soft – you can only
identify it from reddened eyes.
Chopped in little cubes

you lose your power,
transforming them
to childhoods lost

through the cries.
You see, people are so
primitive they named

you after the only colour
they could place, you
became red

 by compromise.[1]

---

[1] People in early societies had a name for black and white and then for red.
The colour of the 'red onion' is, in fact, purple.

ANTHI CHEIMARIOU

*Gravity*


Water is extracted from your freshly
washed linen that hangs there – above
this reflective pool. You watch the sky
and the clouds race one another
like fish fleeing an open-winged
seagull. The only perturbation
of your perfect mirror, a smirr that begins
to make a little turbulence on your
poised illusion. Please believe me
when I say you were made for each other.

# THOMAS CARROLL

## Eyes That Still See

The sun glares.

Sand blows and his last bottle blows with it, fluttering like a flower on the makeshift stalk of its string. Empty. And it has been that way for a day now. He checks the knots again, tight around his belt-loop. He will keep this one till the end.

He walks alone and his feet are cardboard. When the sun is at its highest point they burn with every step. Blistering. Like his face. His cracked lips a map. His salted eyes looking out and looking out and nothing there to see.

Up a rise and down now, carefully upon the slope. His suit jacket is ripped in places. His tailored shirt is gone. What used to be trousers are only ragged scraps below the knee. It is just the little briefcase that is in any good sort of way. He holds it tight and it hangs like an axle for the legs that swing back and forth beside it. Its leather handle has chafed a mountain range of calluses across his hand. The key is on a string around his neck and he brings a hand to it, touching it gently.

Onwards, just movement. If he is going in circles there is no way to tell. Everything is sand and the sand covers everything. Sandsandsandsandsand. Wind in his eyes. Feet going. Legs going. The briefcase in his hand.

The sun draws breaths towards the top of the sky and

at first he is a giant, with limbs that stab and stalk across the sand. Then he is only a little puddle, dripping down the dunes. Another day of this and he might be finished. Three days without water; that was what they had said. No counting.

There is a tree. A withered trunk with limbs splaying out. Beggar. He reaches it and places his briefcase across two of the boughs, creating a mockery of a roof to sit under with crossed arms and crossed legs. It is a cut-out square of darkness among the shimmering light. One full shape. Inside his jacket he finds a tiny crumb of biscuit. Big bright packets on the shelves. Big bright lights and the sounds of people. And trolleys. And the cars all lined up outside in red and yellow and blue. Moving and grasping. Watch it. See it go.

There are bodies and he has gone between them. Husks. Feeding like the desert. Cans, packets, water bottles. Never able to look at the disappearing faces. He has chewed bark from the last living trees. Dug and dug for the hope of anything. He has eaten dead birds and thrown them back up onto the sand.

He was trying.

The sun has moved on. One knee cracks gently as he eases himself up from the ground. He pulls his briefcase off the tree and the wood makes a hollow, scraping sound. A twig snaps off. He flicks it away with his foot and walks.

The earth holds the sun's heat, shifting in discomfort. He high-steps it up a taller dune. Little pebbles dot the smooth surface up and he plucks one from the sand, dropping it in his pocket. It drags there lightly with a weight and a warmness that is strangely comforting. He reaches the top of the rise and studies the drop down.

Not bad. He sits and wraps the case in his arms, sliding and shifting down the slope like he is a sled in winter. He remembers it as he works his way down: their laughs and their smiling faces. Winter. Christmas trees and presents and the open fire.

He reaches the bottom. Stops. Looks back up as if they might be waiting for their turn at the top. He would have cried if tears were not water.

The case takes its usual place. A quick check of the key and the water bottle. This is a flat bit, a vista opening outwards until it becomes a simple hazy line. He walks more and then more he walks until the sun is melting into the ground, smudging the horizon even further. It would have been beautiful on a wall.

Night time. He looks for a place to dig a hole.

Waking reminds him that he is alive. It drags him back to his pains and the sand and each in turn is everywhere. Dry knives at his throat. The third day. The briefcase presses against his sunken belly and he wraps his arms tighter around it. He has to hold them in. Light peeks through one of the holes in his jacket, goading him with little fingers. Go on. Lie down a little longer. Just a little longer now.

Slowly he makes to work himself free of his hole. Sand tumbles down around him and he squirms and rolls and spits – a dog – as the dune collapses. What had been his hole is now folded and sagged and looking more like a big mouth, its tongue lolling out and desperate.

He sits there, waiting. Only the wind moves, a rare cool wind that chills the morning sweat. Fresh like oranges. He closes his eyes to it and smiles, sickly and thin. His legs shake. He is standing somehow, the briefcase still hanging in one hand.

Where? Doesn't matter. It does matter. Away. Anywhere that is not. Just the next step. Just the next ten thousand steps. He feels frail. The briefcase is getting heavier. Spots flash before his eyes.

He will be dead, just like that. Dead like the rest of them. Flies lined up on a windowsill.

Impossible. He sets his teeth and stumbles onwards. There is a slip and crunch as one comes loose. He stops and spits it out into his hand, staring at it. Blood threads in drops down his chin and the sand takes it in greedily. Appetiser. The tooth goes into his pocket with the stone and they scrape against each other as he struggles on.

Light head limp foot heart thrashing like it wants out. Case and bottle and sun and sand and going on and going on. His steps falter and he trips over a dune and down, ending at the bottom in a heap. He looks up. Sand in his eyes. Rubbing. Peering. Ahead of him there is something. He crawls closer and sees the hint of green. The ruffled and glassy surface. It shimmers. It is god. It is the chance of a few more days. Water, its sound and shape and touch, so alien he had almost forgotten it.

One hand reaches back for his hip, but there is nothing. He scrabbles, his fingers searching desperately. The bottle. Gone. His heart thumps. He remembers his tumble down the dune and throws himself upwards in sudden desperate strength.

No bottle. Not after searching for years as his head thunders and the world sways wildly back and forth. He falls to his knees and crawls to the water, his hands pulling closer until his mouth can suck at the edge. He retches and chokes and drinks deeper and slower and shudders, the warmth going all the way down and through him, calming his heart just a little.

Careful minutes of thinking. Sit or leave; one will only be quicker. But, but ... his eyes are drawn to the briefcase. It lies innocently where he had left it, the keyhole watching him with an open eye. The key is there still, around his neck. He takes it off and brings it, shaking, to the lock. An agonizing turn and the deadly snick. The lid opens and brings into the sun the last two pieces of his family. A teddy-bear, droop-nosed, matted. Wrapped around it a necklace, delicate like she had been. Finally crying now, he takes them out and clasps the necklace around his throat. He stares at the teddy-bear, two fingers rubbing at one foot, and then props it up in his top jacket pocket.

He sits there a moment, feeling them. He knows their eyes look down. It is okay. It is all alright. They are going to a new home, far away from this place. He picks up the briefcase and dips it into the water, cupping the fragile liquid. It stays there, beautiful, just so. Now locking it up nice and tight, the key back over his head with the necklace.

Somewhere away from here there is something. It is the only thing that can make any sense. He stands – a little smile, a little promise – his legs pushing himself forwards in a zig-zag line. And water drip-drips from the corner of his briefcase.

TESS SIMPSON

*The Song of the Stone*

Time passes.

It insists on doing that, on marching on, on collecting all kinds of things and throwing them at my feet. As I came into being, slowly, piece by piece, it curled around me like smoke. Stone blocks were heaved into place, coloured glass filtered the light inside, the bells shone and the tower rose tall and strong and all the while, time settled in around me. I did not think it had any affect on me. I was built to shelter; to protect; to shepherd and to warn. I did all those things and I was content.

But then time started to bring me things.

Here is an example:

Once, when I was new in the world, a mother was brought to me. She had a stooped back and a lined face and eyes that stared a hole through the sky. She held a bundle in her arms and had young children clinging to her skirt. She sat with her back against the solid stone of my walls, and then she closed her eyes in my shadow and died.

The children cried, for a while.

I closed my ears to the cries of the children and refused to notice how cold crept over the mother. I thought only of the way they stained my clean expanse. Clouds drifted across the sky.

I do not know where the children went.

Another example:

Time shepherded five men to my door. They were clad in metal and carried swords stained with dark red. They were welcomed and sheltered within my walls, and the next morning they left, to join the river of men marching past me. In the evening, the sky in the distance glowed a dull red. Smoke lingered on the horizon.

Three of the men died that evening. They were buried within my grounds, joining the growing host that found their rest with me. The other two passed by me again on their return home. One lay groaning in pain, the cold night pressing against him like a knife. He was discovered the next morning, stiff and pale. He was buried next to his comrades and was the food for an apple tree who flourished in the garden. It grew from a seed spat out by the final comrade at his wedding. He and his wife had nine children, five of whom came back to rest with me before they were a year old. His wife joined them in place of her ninth child. It was a great many years before the man came to join his family under the earth, and his name continues to this day.

Time tells me these things.

A final example:

A child was left on my doorstep one warm summer evening. He did not cry, not even when he was discovered the next morning. He grew within my walls, quiet and watchful, learned his letters by tracing the names on the stones in my grounds, memorising the words people dedicated to the dead. He wandered my halls at night, when he could not sleep, murmuring those messages under his breath. He hid in the dark, from the men that sometimes came to him in the night. He brushed his hands along my stone, counting his steps. His eyes were quick and bright, flashing like the underbelly of a robin before taking flight. He sang the hymns to himself as he walked. His voice was pleasant.

He ran once. They followed him and brought him back. He found the apple tree, looped a rope around a low, strong branch.

They buried him outside my walls. I can no longer see where he lies. Time brought him to me and then took him away. They all come and leave within a breath of the world and I do not know why they are important.

Time whispers around me. I feel it now as I did not before. Time interferes with my foundations, introduces them to water. It watches as the wind carries off tiny parts of me. It laughs as the people inside me wear me away, footstep by footstep.

I have changed, the people inside me do not know what I once was. Where there was bright colour, now there is grey stone. Where there was beauty, there is now an absence, a lack. I am diminished.

People once used me for shelter, for protection. I held them inside me and barred entrance to those who wished them harm. My halls rang with song and congregations offered up their prayers. They begged for grace and mercy and forgiveness and it was only when they were with me that they felt their voices could be heard. Through my power, they were seen.

They gather so rarely now. I am echoing and empty. Now I am shepherded and protected. They fix and preserve and patch me up with materials that sit on me ill.

And still, time brings me things I do not understand.

You, for example, sitting in my belly. You are wearing blue and red, and you have a camera. I know cameras as I knew the brushes. People used to spend days with me, capturing all of my light, agonising over the stone, the statues, the shadows. They used to hunch, fingers trembling in the cold. They would stretch, brows sweating in the heat. They would spend their time, calculating their resources, making sure that everything was perfect.

You have been here fifteen minutes and have twenty pictures.

I marvel.

Time has brought you here for a reason. I have come to this realisation slowly, over centuries: there must be a reason. There must be some order, some message, some lesson to be learned. Another purpose for me, as I slowly crumble, as I wait for how it must all end. You are here for a reason.

Let me learn it.

Silence reigns. That is unchanged. Whatever else happens outside my walls, as the buildings grow taller and noise takes over the sky, I am silent. The candles flicker, the stone echoes. The bells chime. All is as it was. As it will always be.

You sit, head cocked. Maybe you are listening for something. Once, the chants would have filled the room and made you tremble with their power. Once the bells would have sung. There were celebrations. There were sermons.

You are listening for something. There is nothing to hear. You stand. Are you dissatisfied? Are you waiting?

We are all waiting for something. Me, I wait for the things time brings to my door. I wait for the wind as it smooths away my stones. I wait for the snow, the leaves, the rain. I wait for things to fall.

I was built in preparation for something. I am waiting for something grand, something terrible. Will it come before I am worn away to nothing? The end of it all; will it finally be my purpose?

You are still here. You have been here seventeen minutes. There is enough within me for a lifetime of stories. You haven't ventured into my depths, where the curtains emit dust and damp, where the mice scuttle. You don't know what waits for you there, the secrets hidden and buried. Who lies beneath your feet? Perhaps they are nothing but dust and bone. Perhaps the spirits linger. Perhaps they are simply sleeping. Perhaps they will return to me at the end of everything.

Are you there, little ones? I saw your births, your joys, your sorrows. Will you come back to me at the end?

The clock chimes. It startles you, a dull intrusion. I understand. Time has no respect for the pace of things. It does not wait, it simply goes on.

You are holding something else, I see now. There is a camera in one of your hands, and in the other?

Paper. Black and white. Scrawled handwriting. A picture. An apple tree with a low, strong branch. Is there a connection? A pattern? Is there finally an answer?

Time tells me what but it never tells me why. And yet that is the question they all ask, in their silent prayers. In the quiet and the stillness, in the shelter of stone walls, in the midst of all my history, they always ask me why.

If I could, I would shrug. Time tells me nothing, it only brings me things. It shows me patterns. The rhymes, the chords. Sometimes things happen over and over again.

Seven children, each one buried within me.

Every night, the men come.

The children keep crying.

And sometimes there is you, a person discovering it all for the first time. Though I have been here so long, though the stone you are touching was here when you drew your first breath, will be here when you draw your last, though you make no mark on me, here you are, and I am new again. I am discovered.

I have so many secrets. I am made up of people who have left. I am what remains of them. You are here for the barest moment, but maybe it is enough; there is time left, maybe you could uncover the answers. You have a camera, you have a picture, you have the writing. Just a little longer and it could all mean something. You don't need to leave.

But you do. Of course you do. You look around at the tall, blank walls and trace the letters on one of the plaques, and then you fold the piece of paper and put it away. You go out through the door, the breath of the world in your wake. You were always going to leave, you were only ever going to be here for a moment, and yet I feel the loss. You were only passing through after all.

I hoped I would understand.

A final pattern: the group that appears every afternoon. The people are always different, but the group stays the same. They wander around and they ask questions, and occasionally the questions are interesting. One of the guides has curly black hair and always smiles, even when the group is dull.

'If these walls could talk,' she always says.

What a thing that would be.

It would be a purpose.

You. I would be your purpose.

Stop. Turn back. I have stories to tell.

# M.H. MONICA

## *My First Scooter Lesson (or How I Nearly Launched Myself into Another Dimension)*

Buckle up, folks. I'm going to tell you about the time my grandfather taught me to ride a scooter. Bikes and scooters or mopeds, not to be confused with a motorised scooter, are all the rage in India when you're a teenager.

I was fifteen years old back then, and the prospect of driving on Indian streets terrified me (let me clarify: it still does). On the one hand, we have countless potholes and random pieces of asphalt that stick up like daggers trying to stab wheels and feet. On the other hand, all drivers – of cars, bikes, scooters, trucks, auto rickshaws, and buses – drive like they have countless lives and can respawn as though in a video game. Newsflash, people, you have one life so don't turn your commute to work into a *Fast & Furious* movie.

Despite being scared, I was also excited to learn to drive; it felt like such a 'grown-up' thing to do. So I woke up at dawn, bleary-eyed, during my summer vacation and followed my grandfather to his old, heavy, beaten-down scooter. Once he gathered his faded navy-blue lungi* between his legs and settled his short and sturdy frame onto the seat, he gave me a grunt. Taking the cue, I sat behind him and focused on his white hair, which was slicked back like always, as though he had stepped out of the 60s.

He drove us to a spacious side street where there were hardly any vehicles – just joggers and dog walkers out and about at 6.30am. The Symphony of Honking Automobiles would not begin for another two hours – perfect! My grandfather got off the scooter, handed me the steering, and I thought, *Here we go. Let's zoom around the street.* And then he told me to turn off the engine and start pushing the scooter forward with my feet.

I was confused. Why push it around when you can drive it? But he insisted and so I used every bit of my pre-breakfast energy to push the scooter forward. We made slow progress. And I mean *slow*. He walked by my side, enjoying the cool breeze and slightly swinging his arms while I huffed and puffed like a damn wolf. Sweat quickly gathered on my forehead and back. My limbs were getting tired and a sharp pain started to throb at the base of my spine.

'Why, Thatha**, why?' I asked between gasps.

'It's all part of the process.'

That morning, I deeply empathised with the monks training at Shaolin temples. I was hoping my grandfather wouldn't make me carry buckets of water up the stairs next. Luckily, he told me I was ready to drive after half an hour of scooter-pushing.

He showed me the controls, warned me about the kickback when starting the vehicle, and then gently lowered himself onto the backseat. This made me tremble as I tried to balance the extra weight. Despite his caution, there was a sudden jerk at first, but we held on. And off we went!

I started to enjoy the ride, gaining confidence and speed as I drove. That was when we hit our first obstacle – a speed breaker. I didn't slow down enough, and my poor grandfather and I were lifted off our seats. In that brief moment, mid-air, my short life flashed before my eyes. I saw stars and moons and a bright light calling to me. As we landed back, I was more nervous about how Thatha would react than about the state of our spinal cords. But all he did was grunt at the impact and tell me to steady the steering. Anxiety abated, the ride continued smoothly.

We circled the street a few times, practised driving over speed breakers, *carefully*, and didn't kill any pedestrians. An absolute success of a first driving lesson! He then drove us back home, a proud smile hidden under his thick whiskers. He advised me – as he drove through the dust storms of exhaust – about hand signals, using the side-view mirrors, etc.

We spent a number of days that summer driving around near-empty streets. I started to drive faster, steadier, and he would direct me, grunting every time I hit a speed breaker too hard.

Nowadays, I still hit a few speed breakers occasionally. Old habits die hard. But my life doesn't flash before my eyes anymore. I enjoy the speed; it makes me feel like I'm on a rollercoaster. My initial fears had slowed me down, but no longer.

When I am stuck in the numerous gridlocks of the city, I can easily handle the weight of my scooter without falling over. And boy, do I push and push the scooter with my legs through every possible traffic jam. One would think it is a skill I could use should my scooter break down, but that has not happened even once. However, not a single day goes by where I don't turn off the engine to save fuel and just push forward with ease.

My fear of driving may not have completely vanished, but I drive around everywhere on my scooter now, thanks to Thatha. And I'm sure he's looking down on me, pulling an Oogway from *Kung Fu Panda*, and smiling gently as the wind rushes past me.

*Lungi – Men's casual wear in the Indian Subcontinent. Resembles a kilt and is tied with a simple twist knot

**Thatha – *Grandpa* in some South Indian languages

Our first picture together/my first picture ever

L.K.  KRAUS

*Spirals*

When you step into Grandma's hallway, the first thing you smell is the wooden crockery cupboard in the dining room. My great-grandfather built that cupboard, leaving a memory of careful hands I've never seen on the smooth, nutbrown surfaces. Since then, many hands have scuffed the varnish and polished the edges. There are cups and glasses behind doors with white crochet curtains in front of the tiny windows. These are the doors that get opened the most. Some of the glasses are plastic, green and purple, and when I was little, I drank milk in these colours at breakfast. Memories of tiny hands holding the purple glass, milk trickling down a chin, lie in the deepened wrinkles around Grandma's eyes as she smiles her welcome.

There is a drawer full of cutlery, and two more drawers in which Grandma and Grandpa keep their reading glasses, their linen handkerchiefs, medicines, and a baffling array of anything else you might need, for sending a letter or treating cuts and bruises, mending favourite toys or darning socks. These drawers smell of sage and eucalyptus, leather, starch, and dust. Most things can be fixed when these drawers are opened.

Behind a door on the left, there are compartments with pens and colour pencils and stacks of paper Grandpa used to bring home from work, and all the board games. Treasure maps with wonky skulls and crossbones and gaudy red Xs marking the hollow tree stump in the garden are stacked under the board game boxes. Mixed in with other bits and pieces in a jar is a lucky dice that will roll you a six more often than any other number. Those compartments have a lovely smell, too – like sharpening pencils and the colourful plastic puzzle – but it's only there when you open that door.

There are two doors in the upper part of the cupboard I found out about later than the others, partly because I needed to grow tall enough to reach them first, but also because they don't get opened as much. Inside, there are rows of tiny little glass drawers with enamel labels: *flour*, *sugar*, *cinnamon*, *cloves* and *allspice* on one side, *peas*, *runner beans*, *butter beans*, *sunflower seeds* and *nasturtium* on the other. They don't contain spices or seeds any more. Now, they hold odd coins and buttons that were supposed to get sewn back onto long lost garments, tea lights with charred wicks, a single earclip without its counterpart, a dog biscuit the neighbour with the big curly hairdo left when she visited with her miniature poodle, a faded plastic whistle, a tin frog that used to jump before the key for winding it up got lost, a milk tooth that belonged to one of my aunts or uncles, some passport photos, and a set of playing cards.

The homely smell in the house comes from the tiled compartment where Grandma keeps two kinds of bread, one seeded – 'Grandma-bread' – and one white – 'Grandpa-bread'. The butter dish sits in there, too, next to small saucers of homemade jam.

There is always a clear red berry jam, which Grandma makes from the raspberries, strawberries, cherries, and currants in her garden. She juices them near the old AGA in the cellar, filters the juice through tea towels and boils it with heaps of sugar for hours and hours, the little room sweltering hot when the berries need processing in the summer. Grandma does not allow anyone near the AGA when she's making jam. Happy exhaustion on her face, she watches at the open door, hands on her hips, as her alchemy bubbles away in the pot. The result is a perfect, see-through jam that glows when the light hits it at the right angle. There will also be something yellow, like golden plum or apricot, and something with a stronger flavour, gooseberry, maybe, or even quince, but these are made with the whole fruit, not just the juice. The red berry is everybody's favourite, and when there isn't enough of it to give every grandchild a jar, Grandma reassigns 'favourite' jams with unfaltering confidence. Mine is usually gooseberry. The cupboard taught me the importance of having a good selection of jams in the house, instant summer any time you want it.

Around Christmas, this is where Grandma keeps the gingerbread, too, and over the years the wood has absorbed the memory of it all, a cinnamon-and-honey fragrance mingling with the barley and yeast from the bread.

Today, there is an additional smell weaving through the house. It smells of apples, and I know right away what that means. For as long as I can remember, Grandma has preserved some of the apples from the gnarly trees in her garden by drying them in slices. She does this in her oven overnight, at a low temperature and with a wooden spoon jammed in the oven door to let the steam out. She gets these apples from the cellar, where they wait on a shelf lined with newspaper.

The cellar smells like these apples, and of the earthy outsides of potatoes in a wooden chute, of rubber, coal, and heating oil. Memories of those things linger in the smell of the apples, even now that they're on the dining room table.

There is a knife resting on the kitchen counter, its wooden handle smooth and blackened, the blade worn thin. Grandma never uses a chopping board, she'll cut carrots, green beans, and leeks against her thumb straight over a bubbling pot of soup. This is how the blade came by its crescent moon shape, over years and years of use. When I cut a carrot against my thumb – even if it came from the supermarket in a clean plastic tray – I can smell the rich earth from Grandma's garden, and her care and gratitude transfers into the food I make. I was four years old when I started aspiring to the polished-out rust stains and well-worn look of Grandma's knife and begged my mother to buy me my own. Even now, its blade is still disappointingly straight. Some things can't be rushed.

Grandma picks up her knife now and sits back down at the table to continue peeling apples, each in a single unfaltering, spiralling ribbon of reds and yellows that satisfyingly collapses into the bowl of cores and peel. The apples are wrinkly on the outside and slightly floury on the inside, but not in the bland, mealy way of a bad apple you got from the shop. She gestures for me to take a piece. I sit down and peel one of the apples first, cut it into quarters and offer one to her. She puts her knife down to eat as I choose a piece from her bowl. The apples are flavourful, gentle and sweet, reminders of ripening summer sun and autumn even now, at the beginning of winter, when the air outside is crisp and cold with the smoke of coal-fires adding to its bite. Grandma's liver-spotted hands are steady as she peels, cores, and slices, peels, cores, and slices, committing one more year to memory.

# CONTRIBUTORS

HAYLEY BERNIER (she/her) is a queer writer and editor from Canada. Primarily, Hayley writes poetry, but she is also drafting a novel. She aspires to be a published writer and also a renowned book editor because both of these avenues bring her joy. She is also a fan of vegetarian Scottish breakfasts and rainfall (so, naturally, she often misses living in Edinburgh). In 2022, she was the writer in residence with the nonprofit Literacy in Action, based in the Eastern Townships of Quebec, and she wrote poetry about colonialism and displacement. You can follow her sporadic posts at @burnyayhayley on Instagram.

DAVID BLAKESLEE picks his nose when he thinks no one is watching. He spends a lot of time talking to his cat, and is trying to be less of a book snob. He is most interested in telling stories about ordinary people navigating the many dramas of their everyday lives. Despite his continuous failings, he remains hopeful for his future.

NICOLE CHRISTINE CARATAS is a fiction writer from Chicago. She now lives in Edinburgh, where she is pursuing a PhD in creative writing. Her work has appeared internationally in anthologies and online. She is working on a novel. Find her on Instagram at @_nicolesbooknook and on Twitter at @nicolecaratas

THOMAS CARROLL is an aspiring author living in Edinburgh. When he snatches moments to write in between the rest of life, Thomas tries to propose questions about humanity, life, and the situations that we may one day find ourselves in. Whether it's his longer fiction or shorter pieces, Thomas hopes that the reader will be encouraged to step into the world before them and explore all of its borders.

ANTHI CHEIMARIOU is a poet and editor from Athens, Greece. She holds an MSc in creative writing from the University of Edinburgh and currently works as an editor and the chief communications officer in Eurasia Publications. When she is not sunbathing on a beach in Corfu and is not traveling the world, she writes poetry for independent publications. You can find her at @anthi_ cheimariou on Instagram and LinkedIn.

EMERSON ROSE CRAIG is a writer and editor living in the Pacific Northwest, USA, with an MSc in creative writing from the University of Edinburgh. When not writing her next fantasy story, she works as a contributing editor at *The Selkie* and on the editorial collective for CALYX Press. Her work can be found in *From Arthur's Seat*: Volume 5, *Collection of Mystical Mayhem*, and *Hillfire Anthology*: Volume 1. She can typically be found drinking a large cup of tea and listening to musical theater albums.

JULIANN GUERRA is a prepress coordinator for Scholastic Books from Norwell, Massachusetts. When she is not retelling the most recent rom-com she binge-read to her friends, she's making up scenarios that involve young adults trying to make their way in the world. Some even make it out of her head and onto the page.

JULIA GUILLERMINA is a writer at night, but the daylight turns her into a history teacher. Luckily enough, she lives in Paris, where sunlight is always clouded by a grey veil under which she can hide. She hasn't yet learned how to drop street names in her writing as did The Great, but it's only a matter of time. Until then, you can follow her on Instagram at @julia.gui_ where she plays with words and pictures in English, Spanish, and French.

KATIE HAY-MOLOPO is an aspiring wordsmith from small-town coastal Georgia. Her work often explores faith, the hopeful, the imaginative, and the complexity of being human with other humans. She currently works for One Hundred Miles, an environmental advocacy nonprofit dedicated to loving and protecting the Georgia coast. While she often feels like she's running in a million directions at once, she tries to be grateful for the small things – especially the tugging of her daughter's hand, adventures with her husband, and conversations with the characters of her in-progress YA novel. Learn more at www.hay210.com.

MICHAEL HOWRIE is a failure of all sorts: writing consistently, maintaining deadlines and bowing down to the serial comma. However, the mundane comfort derived from failing in the same way as hundreds of thousands of other literary folks is helpful – for maintaining his bad habits. He currently works as an editor, proofreader and academic educator. Despite these endeavours, he recently sent out an unknown number of job applications in which he claimed to be a professional 'proodreader'. He is very proud of himself.

MIRIAM HUXLEY is a writer and editor from British Columbia who moved to Edinburgh to earn an MSc creative writing (and never left). She recently completed a PhD in creative writing at the University of Edinburgh. She was the 2018 winner of the Sloan Prize for prose in Lowland Scots vernacular and has been published in *The London Reader,*

*From Arthur's Seat, HARTS & Minds,* and *Louden Singletree.* Her other interests involve collecting plants, researching the best vegan cake in the city, and drinking a lot of oat lattes. You can find her on Twitter at @miriamhuxley.

ZALA JAMBROVIC HATIC is a Slovenian writer and editor based in San Diego, CA. She holds an MSc in creative writing from the University of Edinburgh and volunteers as chief editor for *The Selkie* and executive editor for *Hillfire Press.* An avid foodie and a full-time bookworm, she enjoys discovering new fictional worlds as well as creating her own.

ANNA JONES is a travel copywriter by day and a 'fiction writer' by day too, often attempting to do the two things at the same time. Memory, loss, and trauma are some of the cheery themes she likes to explore in her fiction. She is based in the drizzly north of England.

L. K. KRAUS is a writer, editor, and literary translator with connections to Germany, Cornwall and Norway, who lives by the North Sea in Scotland. She is the founder and editor-in-chief of Hillfire Press and the managing director of *The Selkie.* Pursuing a PhD in creative writing at the University of Edinburgh, she is currently working on her first novel. Her work has been published in *Riptide Journal, From Arthur's Seat,* and in the *Together Anthology.* When she is not at her desk, she can usually be found paddling to the Bass Rock and back.

WENDELIN LAW (@wendylawwrites) is a poet and writer born and raised in Hong Kong's concrete jungle. The shadows of its monstrous high-rises haunt her writings – no matter where she goes. She currently lives in Edinburgh – where the rain is a constant downpour of em-dashes. And sometimes, she hears Arthur's Seat roaring like Lion Rock – an iconic mountain in Hong Kong. She is the winner of Verve Poetry Festival Competition 2023. Her manuscript *As Wild As* was shortlisted for *Magma*'s 2022 Poetry Pamphlet Competition. Her poems have also appeared in *Voice & Verse Poetry Magazine, Cha: An Asian Literary Journal*, and elsewhere.

M.H. MONICA fell in love with books at the age of three. With a master's in creative writing from the University of Edinburgh, she is a part-time writer/editor and a full-time daydreamer. Monica has edited and published over 200 books and has written several children's stories for K12 Publications and *From Arthur's Seat*. She is currently supposed to work on her mystery novel but has fallen down a rabbit hole to edit a wonderland of comics. On the odd occasion that she manages to escape, you can find Monica curled up with a good book, movie, show, or anime.

ALEX PENLAND is a museum kid: he spent his childhood running rampant through the Smithsonian museums, which kicked off an early career as a child adventurer. Now a Pushcart-nominated author, he currently lives in Scotland while studying for a PhD in creative writing, where he enjoys reading about quantum physics, playing ukulele, and creating languages in his spare time. His work can be found in *Interzone* and *Metaphorosis* magazine, and his novella *Andrion* was recently published through Knight Errant press. You can follow his work at @AlexPenname on just about any platform, or find his portfolio at AlexPenland.com.

MALINA SHAMSUDIN identifies as a storyteller. Her grown-up stories started in journalism, then public relations for an agency, a multinational, and now, a nonprofit. When not on the hunt for the perfect flat white, this Malaysian can be found grazing on crafty reality TV, talking to dogs, or browsing the children's section of a bookstore.

TESS SIMPSON has been making stories up for as long as she can remember. She started her first novel when she was fourteen and any day now she will finish the third chapter. In the meantime she is a children's bookseller and can often be found yelling about the importance of children's fiction, graphic novels, and translated picture books, as well as about why *Paddington 2* and *Magic Mike XXL* make a surprisingly good double bill. Her work has been published in *From Arthur's Seat* and *Hillfire* Volume 1. If you have a dog, she would love to meet them.

LAUREN N. THURMAN is a writer and editor from Colorado. In both her reading and writing, she embraces moral shortcomings, celebrates abrupt endings, and rejects genre as a concept. She received her MSc in creative writing from the University of Edinburgh and is plodding away at her first novel. Lauren is also co-founder of Lowercase Editorial Services, a freelance editing company supporting businesses and authors.

WREN TRUE is a writer from Des Moines, Iowa. She's been published in *Earthwords*, *From Arthur's Seat*, and the first volume of *Hillfire*. She also has an MSc in creative writing from the University of Edinburgh, and misses the little cafés and sleepy seminars. She likes long naps and bubble tea.

HANNA-MARIA VESTER's (she/they) mission in life is to edit books, write poems, and eat the most delicious food they can find. Besides their obsession with summer rolls, they are absolutely fascinated with the audacity and beauty of poetry. Their writing is currently concerned with endometriosis, gender, relationships, (digital) connection, and memory. Hanna works for an educational publisher based in Germany, but they continually miss the UK. They graduated from the University of Edinburgh in 2020 with a master's degree in literary studies.

SKYE WILSON loves being Scottish. She is a bossy ceilidh dancer, tells everyone The Proclaimers went to her high school, and cries at *Sunshine on Leith*. Skye is slowly learning to be okay with doing things badly. Her poetry is concerned with the body and belonging. Find her on Instagram at @skyegabrielle.

TODD WORKMAN plays with LEGO, rollerblades, has a penchant for staring at the ocean and/or night sky, and dabbles in the forbidden magic of bad puns. An avid student of human nature, he loves misunderstanding basic social interactions and inserting his foot into his verbal facial orifice. He's currently most proud of five poems: his marriage and his four children. While they don't always rhyme and the iambs up tangled sometimes get, the turns never cease to inspire.

ALEXANDRA YE is a full-time dilettante and alleged 'fiction writer' from southern Maryland. She now lives in Edinburgh, where she completed a master's degree in creative writing. Her stories can be found in *Extra Teeth* and *The Offing Magazine*. She is currently doing her best to grow out her hair.

Ingram Content Group UK Ltd.
Milton Keynes UK
UKHW012312210623
423738UK00004B/35